**"YOU DIRTY SON OF A BITCH!"
ROARED RAIDER. "I'LL KILL YOU!"**
He caught Childs full in the heart with a left that sent
him flying back into a frail-looking wooden chair,
splintering it into kindling. But Childs was up on his
feet like a shot, brandishing a chair leg and bringing it
down hard on Raider's head. Blood ran down his forehead and dripped into his eyes as they continued to
pound each other, beating, belting and slamming in a
blazing fire of hatred.

J.D. HARDIN

THE SLICK AND THE DEAD

PLAYBOY PRESS
PAPERBACKS

Published simultaneously in the United States and Canada by Playboy Press, Chicago, Illinois. Printed in the United States of America. Library of Congress Catalog Card Number: 79-83968. First Edition.

Books are available at quantity discounts for promotional and industrial use. For further information, write our sales promotion agency: Ventura Associates, 40 East 49th Street, New York, New York 10017.

ISBN: 0-872-16555-8

First printing November 1979.
Second printing November 1979.

1

The first snow listlessly attacking the earth had been powder dry, creaky underfoot, but with the onset of evening the wind had died and the mercury began climbing out of its ball. Now the flakes stitching the deepening darkness descended larger and wetter, slapping against the windowpane, catching the heat from inside the shack, and sliding down the glass.

Raider tilted the jug high, draining the corn dregs, lowered the jug, and wiped his moustache with his bandanna.

"That ends that."

The burly man fixed to the stool on the far side of the orange-bellied stove glared, grimaced, and spat on the dirt floor. "You empty it, Keough, you fill it."

"In a bit."

Give as good as you get with these boys, thought Raider, *words and deeds. A little respect makes for something like protection.* His eyes strayed from one face to another. The Selkirk brothers, train and stage stoppers, murderers, rape, arson, bank robbery, rustling, horse thieving—name it, they'd done it. Ward, locked to his stool, two hundred pounds of two-legged Brangus bull grinning eager to cut a man up, down, or into chunks, if there was nothing better or more fun to do on a rainy afternoon; brother Jabez, stoop tall, rickety bones crammed into skin the color of dry mustard. And all mouth. As trustworthy as a wounded sidewinder but the quickest hauling iron Raider had ever seen. And needle-eye accurate. The man could shoot a damn barn swallow out from between its wings at a hundred paces. Raider had watched him do it. Lastly there was little brother Aaron, nineteen, maybe twenty, half a dozen neat notches on his gun barrel, not a tooth in his frog face, but a belly for booze any sourdough twice his years would be proud to boast of.

5

He grinned vacantly. "I'll be gettin' thirsty soon, Keough; Ward said it for all of us."

"I'll fetch it when we're done here."

Refilling the jug would mean deserting the warmth of the shack and tramping through the snow most of a mile down the way to the Crowder spread. Old Elon cooked his own corn, kept his toolshed half-filled with jugs—"squeezin's pizen," he called it, fifty cents the jugful, cash and thank you. "And don't stand it too close to a hot stove with the cork in if you don't fancy pickin' chunks o' clay outta yor hide."

Let 'em wait, Raider decided, at least until they started getting fidgety-nasty about it. By then the fourth Selkirk, oldest brother Haber, would be back from Moss Ridge with word as to exactly when the Cheyenne-bound train was due through come tomorrow morning. The rumor was it would be carrying a safe with some ninety thousand in greenbacks neatly strapped and, stacked inside, the Higbe Mines payroll. . . .

Raider's work was cut out and trimmed for him as neatly as a Titusville Fancy Raised-Plaid suit. Collect all four Selkirks and deliver them to the sheriff in nearby Split Cliff, along with sound, stand-up evidence of implication in their previous job—a stage office holdup in Haycomb Springs, two killings, and $32,000 taken. All of this Raider sought to accomplish without losing more blood than he required to stay upright and reasonably alive.

Of immediate concern was the absent Haber. Trailing all four Selkirks down from Haycomb Springs, Raider had outflanked them, allowing them to catch up with him outside of Butler. He had introduced himself as a former associate of Brock Kinsella's. A bigger lie followed, a tall tale worthy of Ananias, of Raider's riding with Kinsella and the Dutchman down around Greeley, getting away when they had come up against a mob of vigilantes, being on his own now, looking to hook up with new partners: "I got the reputation, I got the gun."

The Selkirks had lost a man on the Haycomb Springs job, their cousin Deal. Raider had gone into a long song and jig on how highly Kinsella and the Dutchman held Haber Selkirk. His flattery was outrageous, but it worked and it was welcome stranger.

They were stump stupid these three, the bull, the bones,

and the baby of the brood. But not Haber. Every bunch needed one man to do the thinking, and brother Haber was this bunch's brain. He had ridden out early in the day before the storm. Something he had said just before swinging his mare about and spurring her off had troubled Raider.

"I'll find out the exact time that train's due by and check up on a few other things, like the best getaway route. Might even run into somebody we know. Might run into somebody knows you, Keough. Kinsella and his sidekick was popular gents 'round these parts.

"You run across somebody knew Kinsella, he'd know me for sure," bluffed Raider. "Though by a different name."

"What name?"

"Danaher," he said, "my mother's." It was all smoke, of course, designed to impress Haber with his willingness to play all his cards face up. Raider saw the odds as fifty-fifty. If Haber got to Moss Ridge and did bump into somebody who'd known Brock Kinsella or the Dutchman and he started asking questions, whoever it happened to be wouldn't recall riding with any Danaher or Keough or anybody described as a starved-looking six-foot-two, black eyes, black handlebar moustache, a left-handed gun, wearing a black Stets and hand-tooled Middleton boots.

That would be all Haber would need to smell a dead catfish. Still, the sunny side of the odds said he could ride around the town for ten hours without ever meeting a soul who'd known either Kinsella or his partner.

Jabez was talking, carrying on as he worked.

"Eighty sticks o' Pritchard Red Star dynamite thawed out nicely by settin' 'em ten foot or so from the stove belly like you see here." One by one he picked up the sticks and crumbled them up fine into a copper pot sitting on the seat of a straight-backed chair. Getting to his feet, Aaron pitched in and helped crumble.

"Fetch me that hot water, Keough," said Jabez, indicating the smaller pot on the stove top. Raider obliged. "Hold it steady and pour it into the powder. Not too fast, not too much. The idee is to make it sludgy-like. That's it, now set her on top of the stove. Now with this here wooden spoon I stirs her gentle-like. Looks like porridge, don't she?" Humming tunelessly, he stirred while Raider fidgeted. "There we be. Now off'n the stove and back onto the chair to cool a spell. Aaron . . ."

Aaron nodded, taking a bandanna from his back pocket and handing it to Jabez.

"And that gallon can under the table yonder. Watch this, Keough, it be the critical point. You holt the rag taut like a drum head over the top o' the can." Raider did so and Jabez began spooning the substance onto it, pushing the liquid through with the heel of the spoon. "Litty bit at a time. Whatcha sweatin' fer, Keough, there ain't nothin' gonna happen!"

Spooning it onto the cloth took two full heart-in-mouth minutes by Raider's reckoning until all the dynamite sludge had been pressed through the cloth. Then Jabez wiped his hands on his rear end, flexed his fingers, and, carefully and slowly lifting the gallon can, poured the excess into the pot. "There we be, purty as you please. Sweetest nitroglycerine ever cooked. Aaron, the bottles . . ."

The bottles were two-ounce, wide-mouthed apothecary bottles, four in number. Pinching the lip of the can to direct the flow, Jabez painstakingly filled each bottle in turn, Aaron holding them for him and carrying one at a time to the rear of the shack, where he placed them well back on a shelf.

"Clever, eh, Keough?" asked Aaron grinning at him, displaying his naked pink gums.

"Clever, but . . ."

"What?" inquired Jabez, carrying the can with what was left in it to the table and setting it underneath out of harm's way.

"We're at least two miles from Moss Ridge. How do we get the soup over there by horse with all the jouncing and bouncing without blowing whoever's carrying it sky high?"

"We-uns ain't worried none 'bout that," said Ward, breaking his silence and leering. "We got us a vol-yun-teer fer thet little chore."

Raider sighed. "Guess who."

"You guess right. Now you've had yer lesson in how to cook soup, how's about gettin' yer ass up off'n thet chair, haulin' it down the way, and gettin' thet thar jug refilled?"

"Ward, if I got to do the fetching, I got a right to ask questions. What do we need nitro for anyhow? Me and

Brock and the Dutchman never used it. Too dangerous. We can blow those train tracks with black powder, better yet dynamite. . . ."

"You can't blow the safe with no dyne," countered Jabez. "Oh, you can, but you're apt to blow it through the roof and scatter the money to hell and gone. Nitro's easier to control."

Aaron nodded. "Old Habe even uses it to bust couplings."

"Far as you being the one to carry it over to Moss Ridge, you got no cause to sweat. Aaron there carried twice't as much halfways 'cross Montana Territory last fall."

"Up over the Bitter Root range," added Aaron proudly. "Ten whole bottles in my saddlebag."

Jabez nodded. "Just you ride easy, slow 'n steady, without your horse trippin' or fallin'. You'll be fine. And once we stop that old train you'll be in for a right good show. Mister, brother Habe can open a safe with soup slicker 'n quicker than you can pee down your leg into yer boot!"

"I still say . . ."

"Say shit!" snapped Ward, rising. "Just you get aholt thet jug and go get it filled like I told you. You may be tight with Brock Kinsella and that blowbelly buddy o' his, but you ain't no full-fledged member o' this here outfit yet. You got yer 'prenticeship to sarve afore you can call yerself a equal one to the Selkirks. Now stir your stumps!"

Raider picked up the jug and unlatched the door, the wind forcing it out of his grip and sending it clattering against the inside wall, the snowfall rushing in, hissing against the stove. He pulled and Jabez pushed to close it. Head down, boring into the wind with the crown of his Stetson, Raider trudged through the drifts, making his way to the ramshackle shed that served as a stable. Clearing the snow from the door front with his boots, he unlatched the door, swung it wide, fumbled about inside for the lantern, found and lighted it, and hung it on a nail. Taking his time, he began saddling the bay. Intercepting Haber was an absolute must, even if it meant a showdown. Damnit, suddenly everything was busting apart at the joints! He'd originally planned to ride out on the job with all four and bust it up right in the midst of things, catch the whole bunch off guard, take Haber hostage, gun to his head, order the rest to throw down their arms, ride them to the nearest law, and turn them in.

Mounting up, he started for Crowder's, his jacket collar tight about his neck. Maybe he shouldn't hold off until the job. It might make more sense to try and split them up, take them two at a time. But how?

The snow had stopped falling and the sky was beginning to clear, the blue clouds tearing apart to reveal the winter moon pouring its cold light over the whitened world.

He had covered nearly a hundred yards, the horse high-kneeing the drifting snow and shivering with the cold, when he spotted a figure far ahead breaking the line separating white from black with a steady up-and-down motion. Man and horse coming straight at him. No. Squinting, shading his eyes from the moon, he could see two men and horses, one following the other.

Complications. . . . Great, this was all he needed. Four against one, now five. He was riding with his reins in his right hand, left forearm holding the empty corn jug against his belt. Now his left hand moved to his .44, easing it free of its leather, letting it hang straight down, and practicing tilting the barrel up to firing angle. Up and down. Up and down. Out and ready; that was it. Neither rider would be able to spot it on the off side, concealed as it was by his body.

The distance between the two and the one shortened as the yellow light in Crowder's front window grew larger, stronger, drenching the snow heaped up under the glass, turning the silver crystals to gold. Now barely twenty yards separated Raider from the oncoming pair. The man in the lead waved and called. Haber . . .

"Hey, yah . . ." He reined up, his horse rearing its head, snorting, great clouds pouring out of its nostrils, curling away left and right. The other man stopped behind him; Raider rode up to them.

"It's Keough. I'll be damned." Haber turned to the other man, then back to Raider, as if to assure himself that his companion was paying attention. "What's up, Keough?"

Raider raised the empty jug. "Getting a refill from Crowder." He brought it back down, his eyes fixed on the stranger's round, red face, the eyes slits neatly cut under the brim of his hat. Having eased his mount around to Haber's left side, he was staring at Raider, his eyelids parting, his eyes glinting curiosity. Taking the good look.

It was all Raider needed. Tossing the empty jug at Haber, who caught it in a reflex action, Raider brought up his .44 and leveled it at him. "Freeze, both of you."

"What the hell . . ." began Haber.

"You, with the whiskey nose, swing around and get the hell out of here."

"Hold on," snarled Haber.

"Move. You, Haber, drop the jug and get 'em up, fingers locked over your hat."

"Haber . . ." began the other.

"I'm counting to ten, you, then I shoot. If you're in range you're dead. One . . . two . . ."

The man muttered, flashed an angry look at Haber, swung about, roweled his horse's flanks, and rode off billowing loose snow behind him.

Haber studied Raider. "Your brain snapped or something? Is that it?"

"Just playing it safe."

"Real cute, ain'tcha, I mean real brainy cute, slick talking us into letting you ride with us. Pretty stupid, claiming you rode with Kinsella and the Dutchman, though. What in hell made you think I wouldn't check up on you?"

"You think you were smart, telling me you were gonna?"

Haber spat and, unlacing his fingers, started his hands down over his hat brim. "As if you didn't know I would——"

"Up on your hat and keep 'em there."

Haber complied. "You know you're dead," he said evenly. "You know that, don't you? Who you working for, anyhow? That hayseed sheriff over to Haycomb Springs?"

"Nope."

"Who?"

"None o' your goddamn business."

"Suit yourself. So what do we do now, sit out here jawing till our assholes freeze and clank off?"

Raider urged his mount forward a stride, seizing the

other's rifle out of its boot, cradling it in his free left fore-arm, then slipping it into his own empty boot.

"Bring your left hand down across your front, ease your gun up and out, and drop it. One dumb move and I'll kill you."

"Horseshit! You fire that thing, the boys'll be out here in two seconds. They'll cut you into halves quicker'n you can wink your eye!"

"Do it."

"Okay, yeah . . ." The pistol dropped heavily, outlining itself perfectly in the snow. "Now what?"

"Now we ride back to Split Cliff. And I introduce you to the sheriff."

Cocking his head to one side, Haber eyed Raider. "Who was it you said you're working for?"

"I didn't." Raider lifted his lariat from his saddle. "Swing around, hands down and behind you." Haber hesitated, then obeyed. "Wrists together." After looping and tying his wrists securely with one end of the rope, Raider strapped the other twice around his own right wrist, leaving twenty feet free between. "Now swing around to your left and head back. We'll be going 'round the shack by the well to pick up the sack, then up the hill to town."

They started out. "You looking for money?" asked Haber. "I mean man-sized money, enough to keep you in whores and Tangleleg whiskey for the next twenty years? You got it. I'll give you half o' what's in that Wells Fargo sack. Sixteen thousand bucks."

"Why half? I can have all of it."

"You wouldn't do that. That's stealing. We busted our backsides for that money!"

"Sure you did."

"Who you working for?"

"Just ride, a nice steady gait, just like you're going. No dumb plays."

One following the other, they circled the shack wide and, coming up the side, had approached to within a few feet of the well when the front door suddenly opened, throwing light out onto the snow. Somebody—because of the angle Raider couldn't make out who—looked out.

"One sound and you're dead," he whispered to Haber.

Brief, indistinguishable conversation followed among those inside the shack and the door closed. Their thirst

2

Lamps large and small, dim and glaring, challenged the gloom down the length of the snow- and mud-covered main street separating Split Cliff. As was customary on the heels of sundown, the piano in the Crystal Slipper fell victim to a merciless manhandling, sending forth the tortured strains of "Rye Whiskey," the music accompanied by a collection of well-soaked voices of varying tones and qualities, with occasional loud female laughter providing cacophonous counterpoint. Traffic slogged and trundled up and down, pedestrians and stray dogs darting between vehicles and horses, and along the wooden sidewalk in front of the General Store a fistfight rapidly degenerating into a wrestling match was drawing a sparse but enthusiastic audience.

His prisoner leading him at the knotted end of the rope, Raider passed a small covered wagon, its rear wheels half again the size of its front ones, a wooden sign fastened to its side: "Acme Overland Apothecary. If you're ill, if you ail, AOA will never fail." A mule attired in a plaid blanket occupied the wagon shafts, and a derbied gentleman wrapped in a covert box mackintosh against the night chill held the reins, a long and comically crooked cheroot clamped in his bicuspids.

Raider and Haber approached the hitching rail in front of the sheriff's office opposite the apothecary wagon. They were dismounting when the man at the mule's reins slapped the creature's rump one time and started down the street.

"Friend of yours?" inquired Raider.

"Never seen him before in my life."

"I hope that's a fact, for both your sakes."

The sheriff's office, boasting a two-cell jail in the rear, was small but cozy, a solid oak curtaintop desk against one wall, three split-bottomed chairs, and a gun rack holding two new Winchesters and a worse-for-wear Henry against the other wall. The Henry's stock displayed a crack running nearly its full length, doubtless put there, thought Raider, by some peace-disturbing drunk's skull. In each of the cells stood a wooden bed with a shock mattress and a frayed-edge army blanket neatly folded at the foot.

The man behind the badge occupying the chair at the desk was doorway-broad, big-boned, and well muscled and smelled of tobacco and rye. He wore his pewter-gray hair long, Custer-style, and the features it framed looked as if more than a few fists had attempted to alter or rearrange them. Raider introduced them both, handing over his identification.

"Pinkerton, eh?" said the sheriff with surprise in his reedy voice. "What you doing out here? I allus thought you fellers worked 'round cities."

"I'm on assignment for Wells Fargo." Raider set the sack on the desk, opened it, and poured out the contents. "Thirty-two thousand, count it."

"Holy Toledo!"

"Taken from the depot safe in Haycomb Springs. This guy and his three brothers."

"Where's the others?"

"Murdered!" snapped Haber. "In cold blood. He blew 'em to kingdom come. Most brutal thing you ever seen. He's the one oughta be jailed, not me!"

Raider filled the sheriff in on the particulars over Haber's persistent interruptions, adding: "You might send somebody out to collect the pieces and bring in their horses."

"First thing in the morning," responded the sheriff. "They sure enough ain't goin' noplace. How long do I got to hang on to this one?"

"Two or three days at most. He'll be picked up and taken back to Goshen County for trial on the Haycomb Springs charge. They killed two people."

"I didn't kill a damn soul!" burst Haber. "It was Ward done it. Him and Aaron does all the killing."

"Talk 'em into confessing, Haber," said Raider. "You'll be ahead of the game." He turned back to the sheriff. "I'll be going along now, if you don't mind."

"Where you staying? I might want to get in touch with you."

"Equality House."

"For how long?"

"That's hard to say. Tonight for sure, maybe tomorrow, maybe a week. Depends what comes up. I might have to go back to Haycomb Springs to testify. I write up my report and it's wired in . . . generally that's all that's needed. It should be this time, seeing they got a sackful of evidence to go along with it. That reminds me, I got to have a receipt."

The sheriff found a pencil stub in his bottom drawer, selected a piece of paper from his wastebasket, made a half-hearted effort to smooth it, wrote the receipt, and signed it with a flourish.

"Thanks." Raider turned to Haber. "So long, Haber, it's been a pleasure."

"Go fuck yourself, Fink Pinkerton! And keep a weather eye on your ass while you're at it. Ain't nobody going to hang this old boy. I'll get away and I'll be coming after you. You're going to die with more pain than any man on earth ever felt, I promise you!"

"Whatever you say. Just don't be disappointed if you've got to wait in line for a crack at me."

The temperature could not seem to find a level to satisfy itself for the night, and by the time Raider had finished turning his prisoner and Wells Fargo's money over to the sheriff, the mercury had plummeted. The last clouds rolled away, leaving the moon and a clutch of gelid-looking stars in attendance upon it. A bitter, biting wind came up, a noisy invisible brawler surging about rattling windows, testing tree branches, and battling its way into Raider's marrow.

Two miles out of Split Cliff the skin of perspiration separating his body from his clothing began to chill viciously, his teeth seemed to shrink in his mouth as they started chattering, and the freezing air began aching his nostrils clear up to his hairline.

Ahead, just beyond a fork in the road, a grove of trees sprouted from the snow-snugged land. In their midst stood the covered wagon earlier parked across the street from the sheriff's office. The blanketed mule had been

freed from its shafts and was standing behind the largest tree out of the wind. There was, however, no sign of
the man in the derby. Raider rode up to the wagon, dismounted, walked around to the tailgate, and peered inside. The man was fussing with a kerosene lamp. He
glanced up.

"What's been keeping you?"

"I've been jawing with the law."

"Something's wrong with this lamp; it keeps dying on
me."

"Ever think of trying a new wick? That one must be
seven years old." Pulling himself up over the tailgate,
Raider sat down on a crate stenciled "Dr. Wheatstone's
Asthma Cure," tilting his hat back and pulling off his
gloves, flexing his fingers. "Jesus, it's cold out there."

The other man's thumbnail snapped the head of a lu-
cifer, igniting it. He thrust it inside the glass, bringing
the lamp to life. Trimming the flame, he set the lamp on
a nearby chest and sat down opposite Raider.

"So what happened? How come you only brought in
one Selkirk? What did you do with the others? Did they
get away? How?"

"Come on, Doc, one question at a time." Raider sighed
and yawned, raising his numbed fingers over the chimney
of the lamp. Flexing them, he began relating what had
happened. The longer he talked, the more impatient the
other became, frowning, fidgeting, and shaking his head
in disapproval.

"Man, you really botched this one up, didn't you?"

"What in hell are you talking about?"

"Blowing up three out of four isn't botching it?"

"I had no goddamn choice, *Mister* Weatherbee! Let
me tell you something, rolling that rock down was pretty
quick thinking. Smart!"

"Brilliant. The big bosses back at the Agency ought
to be very impressed."

"It saved my life."

"They'll appreciate that, I'm sure."

"You tell 'em what happened like I'm telling you and
they can't help but see the sense of it."

"What I fail to understand is why you let it get this
far?"

"What far? What are you talking about?"

"You had all four cold when you caught up with them coming down from Haycomb Springs. Why didn't you take them then? Why hold off until Moss Ridge?"

"Use your head, for chrissakes! What good would bringing them in then do us?"

"They had the money on them, didn't they?"

"Sure, but you get 'em up before judge and jury, and sure as shooting three would finger the fourth for stealing it. Three out of four would go scot-free!"

"On top of two murders? You must be kidding! Let me smell your breath."

Raider clenched his teeth and fought down the anger boiling up inside. He was cold, hungry, thirsty, exhausted, and deep down as disappointed in the way things had turned out as the fault-finding, cheroot-chewing man facing him. But he wasn't about to agree that he'd botched things up. As he explained, his original plan had been to thwart the Selkirks in the midst of the Moss Ridge train robbery, with fifty passenger witnesses practically breathing down their dirty necks.

"That way there'd be no way they could wriggle out of it." He pounded his knee with each word. "That sack from Haycomb Springs just wasn't enough!"

"All right, don't get all heated up neurotic."

"You got to remember, there wasn't one stinking one-eyed witness to the Haycomb Springs job. All I had was my suspicions till I caught up with 'em and spotted the sack. I used my head all the way, every move, every step. . . ."

"What made you tell the ringleader, what's his name . . . ?"

"Haber. That I ran with Kinsella and the Dutchman? Why not? One bunch is as good as another."

"You could have told him the Pierce gang over near Cole Flats, or some of those crazies down by the border. Why pick somebody in the Selkirk's own backyard, somebody they could check up on in two shakes? And did."

"Goddamn you, Weatherbee, you bust my nuts, you really do! You sit there carping and criticizing. . . . I do all the bullwork, all the sweating, all the straining, while you run around in this goddamn wagon peddling stomach junk to anybody dumb enough to buy it, no gunplay, no chasing, no risk. Me, I walk into the lion's mouth four against one——"

"Simmer down, Rade."

"You got some almighty fucking gall!"

"You're forgetting one thing. You asked me straight out to stay out of this one. You said this was a one-man infiltration; two bodies would ruin it for sure. You wanted it that way, I let you have it."

"Let me? Who in hell are you all of a sudden, Allan Pinkerton?"

"You know what I'm saying . . ."

"I know shit!"

"I believe you!"

"How would you like a goddamn busted jaw and twenty teeth down your windpipe?"

"How would you like to try it? But before you do, before I bloody you up and knock you colder than outside, get your gloves back on, get up that pole out there, and cut me into the line."

Ignoring Raider's loud and blasphemous response to this suggestion, Doc rose from his seat and pushed it toward the front of the wagon. Pulling a twenty-inch square section up out of the wagon bed, he brought up battery jars, a transmitting apparatus, and a receiver. Hooking up a coil of rubber-insulated wire, he handed the free end to Raider.

"Up you go . . ."

"That's another thing, how come I always got to do the damn dirty work?"

"Because you're so good at it. Go on, get up while I set things up."

Raider cursed, spat, scowled, pouted, and muttered something to the effect that Mrs. Weatherbee's only son was a mackintoshed fancy-drawers incapable of climbing ten feet of stairs let alone shinnying up a naked pole in freezing weather with a high wind howling up his hind end.

Emerging from the wagon, he discovered that the high wind had managed to heighten itself appreciably during his respite from it. Taking the wire between his teeth, he started up the pole. When he reached the insulator, he wrapped his legs tightly to lock himself in place, removed his gloves, and connected the wire to the line. His hands were out of his gloves for a few seconds only, but in that brief period they turned pink, then red, and were threatening purple by the time the job was completed. Sliding down and climbing back into the wagon, he found Doc testing his instrument.

"Cross your fingers the line isn't broken," he said. "We've got almost a thousand miles between here and the Chicago office."

"Where are you going through?"

Doc reached into a nearby satchel, took out a map, and unfolded it with one hand. "Sioux City, then Dubuque."

"You'd better encode."

"Are you telling me my business?"

"I'm telling you Pinkerton Agency business isn't anybody else's."

"There's no need to worry how I report your colossal botch-up. Just sit back and think about what Wagner's going to tell you when he hears about your snowball fight."

"It was no such thing and you know it!"

But Doc wasn't listening. He had stopped transmiting almost immediately he'd started. Exploring the satchel again, he came up with a small black book. "On second thought maybe I ought to write it up and encode it."

"Lucky thing somebody tells you your business, Mr. Know-it-all." Raider wiped his mouth with the back of his glove. "You got anything to drink in this broken-down mule surrey?"

"Everything. Dr. Echol's Australian Aurilco Wonder Heart Cure, Hammond's Blood Purifier and Invigorator, Brown's Vegetable Cure for Female Weakness, falling of the womb, leukorrhoea, irregular and painful menstruation, flooding . . ."

"You're comical as snakebite, you know that?"

"Snakebite? I've got . . ."

"Oh, shut your mouth!"

Doc's laugh was forced and loud as he set about writing up the report with Raider correcting practically every other sentence. The information was then encoded and sent away to the Pinkerton Chicago office.

"How can you be sure you got through?" inquired Raider.

"How many times have you asked me that? And how many times have I told you I can't, not until he gets back to me." Doc paused and glanced about the cramped confines of the wagon. "Listen to that wind. It wouldn't surprise me if its pulled down half the poles from here to the Nebraska line."

They waited in silence, Raider nursing his thirst, Doc whistling patiently, much to his partner's irritation, both men's eyes on the receiver, each man mutely urging it to come to life. The wind sustained its harsh and discordant aria, the wagon bonnet all but ripping under its relentless buffeting like sails in a hurricane.

"How about your mule?" asked Raider. "My horse can take cold, but . . ."

"Don't worry about Judith. She can stand cold seven times stiffer than you can. She did up around Flathead Lake in Montana two years ago. That was cold, with a wind strong enough to blow one barn inside another."

"Still we ought to get 'em both inside, fed and warmed up."

"Soon as we hear."

The receiver clicked uncertainly, stopped, clicked again, and began chattering.

"What's it say? What's it say?" blurted Raider.

"Sssssh. Report . . . received . . . acknowledged . . . message . . . follows. . . . Hand me that pad and pencil by the lamp, quick."

The receiver continued clicking away as Doc hunched over it, scribbling. The message was brief, transmission ceased abruptly, he acknowledged, speedily decoded, and began restoring his equipment to its hiding place under the floorboards.

"Well, what in hell did he say?" snapped Raider.

Doc beamed. "New assignment. Amarillo."

"Texas! Beautiful! Good-bye winter!" Raider cheered lustily.

"We'll have to close up shop here first thing in the morning. I'll have to shoot my pictures for the Selkirk–Haycomb Springs case journal, all those people, dead and alive." He scanned the map. "We've got a good five-hundred-mile ride ahead of us."

"At the rate you and this rig travel, it'll be a good slow ride. How about if I ride on ahead and set things up?"

"How about we ride together. Put your gloves on."

"What for?"

"We've got a wire up out there. You get back up and disconnect it."

"The hell with it. Let's just snip it off and leave it."

"Rade . . ."

"Okay, okay, you and your dumb damn wires and bottles and click, click, click. Jeez, I'm thirsty!"

3

The anteroom was filled with the heavy and sickening fragrance of lilac—or lavender, something whorey-smelling, Raider couldn't decide what specifically. It was so powerful it completely smothered the scent of a bouquet of freshly cut yellow roses stuffed in a cut-glass vase on the table opposite where they were sitting. The Seth Thomas clock on the wall above the bouquet clicked off another minute of the morning. Doc sighed impatiently, checked his watch against the clock, and started drumming one knee with the brim of his derby.

"Don't do that!" whispered Raider irritably.

"Why not?"

"It makes me nervous."

"Sorry."

"This place makes me nervous; that ungodly stink. That's the powder they use, you know."

Doc nodded sympathetically but deliberately resumed his rapping, embellishing the beat by cleverly switching knees every third rap. Raider was on the verge of snatching his hat from him and separating the crown from the brim when the drapes filling the way into the adjoining room parted to reveal a cadaverous-looking Amarilloan affecting a pair of offset guard spectacles and a newly sprouted beard. His restless pink fingers wandered about his upper body seemingly in search of a place to hook on.

"Gentlemen, I'm afraid Mr. Sessions is quite busy and won't be able to come out. He said to tell you either come back tomorrow or, if your business is urgent, step inside and discuss it with him while he's working."

"We'll come back tomorrow," said Raider.

"We'll step inside," said Doc.

"Doc, I got no stomach to watch an undertaker working, I really haven't."

Doc stood up. "Rade, I'll explain to you one time and

24

hope that it sinks in. This is a brand spanking new case. We're supposed to be on the track, but it looks to be getting colder by the hour. We're in no position to delay matters another whole day."

"Okay, okay, but don't blame me if I upchuck into your goddamn hat!"

The odor permeating the preparation room of Sessions & Sessions Funeral Parlors, Amarillo's Finest Burials, was distinctly unlike that of the anteroom. This was a brutally acrid stink that lanced up Raider's nostrils with the suddenness of injection needles, chasing down his throat and into his already somewhat upset stomach.

Texas sunlight coming in through three large windows flooded the room. To the left as they entered was a large wooden cabinet with glass doors, its shelves cluttered with scalpels, scissors, forceps and augers, clamps, needles, pumps, tubes, bowls, and basins. Marshaled together on the top shelf with the overflow occupying the top of the cabinet itself were bottles and tins, an imposing array of fluids, sprays, pastes, oils, powders, and creams designed to repair or soften tissue, shrink or enlarge it, dry it, color it, moisten it—whatever the artist desired. Cosmetics, waxes, and paints were scattered about the room on small tables, and on the floor hard by the cabinet sat a large bucket conspicuously labeled plaster of Paris.

But it was neither supplies nor equipment that drew and held Raider's unappreciative eye, rather the long wooden table in the center of the room and the naked cadaver occupying it, wearing matching purple holes in the epigastric region of its sunken chest.

Doc introduced the two of them to Mr. Wilton W. Sessions, proprietor, with his brother, and master cosmetician of the establishment. "A Leonardo of the lifelike," "a Rembrandt at restoration" were among the compliments Doc immediately began lavishing upon the man—much to his partner's annoyance and disgust. Doc's effusive praise prompted Sessions to immediately launch a running commentary on the task confronting him in preference to inquiring as to the nature of their visit.

"I've already cleansed and disinfected the gentlemen's skin and hair and, as you see, closed the mouth and the eyes. Notice the beatific expression."

Doc nodded. "He looks very contented."

"He was scared out of his boots, tensed up and bug-eyed. I sculpted that serene look. *Requiescat in pacem.*"

"Ever see anything so artistic in your life, Rade?" Doc turned to his partner.

"No . . ."

"That's one thing that has to be done right away," commented Sessions. "Before rigor mortis sets in."

Raider wanted no part of either watching Sessions's skills in application or conversation regarding them. He made his way to the chair standing furthest from the table, slumped down into it, and turned his face to the window, fighting back the nausea threatening to dislodge his breakfast.

Mr. Sessions selected a needle from a porcelain tray, filled it from a large bottle, and held it upright. After opening an artery with a small scalpel, he proceeded to empty the contents of the needle into the body.

"What's that for?" inquired Doc, his interest completely captured by the proceedings.

"Who gives a sh—— who cares?" piped Raider without looking. "What are we wasting the man's time for? Why can't we get to what we came here for?"

"Pay no attention to my friend, Mr. Sessions," said Doc. "The only flaw in his otherwise exemplary character is a notorious lack of patience."

"This fluid inhibits the clotting of the blood," announced Sessions. "It helps drain it off and prepares the vein for injection of the arterial fluid, the preservative."

Picking up a second needle, Sessions injected the arterial fluid, hooking up a hand pump to ensure sufficient pressure for proper distribution.

"Good God . . ." rasped Raider as the pump began working and he tore his eyes away from the window long enough to see what was going on.

Sessions worked on, disclosing in passing that the unfortunate occupant of the table had rashly called a prominent local citizen a liar in front of sixty-odd witnesses, incurring the man's resentment and acquiring two bullets from the insulted one's .45 in consequence. The undertaker was in the midst of the final phase, injecting cavity fluid, when, unable to stand it any longer, Raider lurched to his feet and interrupted:

"Doc, will you for crissakes forget about that—that deceased on the table and get on about ours."

His partner eyed him icily and, turning to Sessions, apologized and explained their reason for being there.

"We've already talked to the sheriff. He tells us the deceased's name was Grater. He was manager of the local Wells Fargo office."

"That he was," said Sessions. "They brought the body in less than half an hour after the safe was broken into."

"They got eighty-five thousand," interposed Raider in an obvious effort to hurry things along. His face was ashen and he was breathing deeply, clearly battling the urge to vomit.

Sessions shurgged, mopping his bald head with his handkerchief and putting away his needle. "That I wouldn't know. My only interest was in the deceased."

"The sheriff said his head was missing," said Doc.

"Yes. When they brought him in here, his neck looked like raw beef. A miserable job of decapitation, though. Whoever did it must have used an ax."

"No ax, hatchet, cleaver, nothing like that was found at the scene," commented Raider.

Doc nodded. "We searched the office from top to bottom. I took fifty-two photographs of everything from every conceivable angle. Evidently no cutting instrument of any sort was seen by anyone."

Sessions pulled a sheet over the corpse, crossed to the washstand, and began to soap his hands.

"I started on the body just a few minutes after it was brought in. Pretty much what you saw me do here, along with plastering up the neck." He paused, a frown tightening his plain features. "Come to think of it, one thing struck me funny about that." His interest aroused, Raider got up and joined the two of them at the washstand. "Sam had lost a lot of blood before I got him. I'd say sixty to seventy percent drained. You'd have imagined whoever decapitated the poor fellow had hung him up by the heels."

"Mind if I smoke?" inquired Doc.

"Go ahead."

Doc produced an Old Virginia cheroot, offering one to Sessions, who declined it with a wave. Lighting up with great ceremony, Doc blew ceilingward and continued: "You knew the deceased personally."

"As well as I know my own brother."

"What sort of man was he?"

"Quiet, just about the most closed-mouthed human be-ing you'd ever run into. He was a widower; lost his wife about two years ago. Her sister kept house for him."

"Did they get along?"

"As far as I know."

"Did he get along with people in general?"

"With everybody. Sam Grater didn't have an enemy in the world."

"Maybe one," commented Raider wryly.

"Did he and his wife have any children?" Doc went on.

"No."

"Is his sister-in-law still around town?" asked Raider.

"Nope. She lit out for St. Louis right after the funeral. Told me straight from the shoulder that she wouldn't stay in this town, in that house, for a million dollars."

"You don't happen to know her address in St. Louis, do you?" inquired Doc.

"No. I doubt anybody does here. She broke clean with Amarillo."

"What was her name?" asked Raider.

"Alice Dickerson. Old maid. Not old really, in her early fifties, I'd guess, but never married. She identified the body. Fainted dead away doing it. I couldn't blame the poor woman. Sight of somebody you know that well without his head is no sight to see."

Raider nodded. "Can you remember offhand what Grater was wearing?"

"Sure. We buried him in just what he had on that night. Black wool suit, blue bow tie, black button shoes. Sam never was much for boots. He was no real Texan at heart."

"Any jewelry?" asked Raider.

"Masonic ring, pearl cufflinks, silver belt buckle." Sessions paused and stared fixedly. "That's funny, too. His tie and collar, now I think about it, I didn't see a speck of blood on either one, or on his coat shoulders either, for that matter."

"Should there have been?" asked Raider. "I mean what's your professional opinion on that?"

"Your friend here is a doctor," said Sessions. "Ask him."

"He's no medical doctor," replied Raider. "Just a bottle juggler."

"I am a purveyor of patent medicines," said Doc, "duly licensed and qualified." He glared at Raider.

"Well, I don't have any professional opinion on cold-blooded murder. I don't get 'em in the act, only after. But since you ask, I expect it is possible he could get his head chopped off without spilling any blood on his clothing. Stranger things have happened."

"He'd have to be lying down when they did it," ventured Doc, "which would mean he'd been hit over the head first."

Sessions shrugged his puny shoulders. "Without his head to examine, there's no way of telling for sure."

"I got a wild thought," said Raider. "You don't suppose he opened that safe himself and blew his head off doing it, do you?"

"Hardly," responded Doc. "I can't imagine any man blowing a safe he knows the combination to."

"He might if he wanted you to think outsiders did it."

"If he did, Rade, who do you figure ran off with the money—mice?"

"I said it was a wild thought, didn't I?"

"Not as wild as it is stupid."

"If you suspect Sam of stealing his own money, you're way off the track," announced Sessions firmly. "The man was honest as the preacher."

Doc nodded. "I'm sure. I take it you socialized with him."

"You bet. Same friends, same lodge, same church. We saw a lot of each other."

"How long had he been in charge of the Wells Fargo office here?"

"Years and years."

"We keep a journal," said Doc, "all the information on a case. Every case. According to what we've been able to gather on this one so far, most of it turned over by the Wells Fargo people, their office here in Amarillo has never been robbed before. To your knowledge, is that a fact? I'm asking you because the sheriff is new in town, employees come and go, and you've been around awhile. . . ."

"Fifty-six years. No, I can never remember the office being robbed before." Sessions paused and began rapping his chin with his index finger. "Can I ask you something?"

Doc nodded. "Ask away."

"Having his head cut off and missing like it is, is that a clue?"

"If it is, it beats me," said Doc. "Well, we've taken enough of your time. We appreciate your help."

"Thank you kindly," said Raider. He looked about. "I got to hand it to you, I don't know how you can do this work."

"I enjoy it," said Sessions, his chicken chest swelling with pride.

Raider stared at him, but said nothing.

"Keep me posted, will you?" asked Sessions. "I expect Wells Fargo's only interested in getting their money back, but I sure hope you find out who killed Sam."

"We find one, we'll find the other," said Doc. "Good day to you, sir."

4

"What's your line o' work, handsome?" She turned from the oval mirror, directing her naked body at him and searching his eyes for a glimmer of favorable impression.

"I work very hard at doing as little as possible," answered Raider, reaching across the pillow for the bottle of Forty-rod. "You got some figure, you know that, Miss Floraday?"

"I told you my name is Rouge. All my friends call me Rouge. It's French for red."

"Some figure . . ."

"Well, you got yourself some fine tallywhacker, Mr. O'Toole. And you sure know how to use it. After you on the spirits, thank you."

"Ladies before gentlemen." Raider passed her the bottle. She palm-wiped the top, downed six swallows, opening his eyes wider with each successive one, and handed back the bottle, which Raider relieved of its remaining contents with a single healthy swig. It was like a torch jabbed down his throat, bitter as gall and tarantula-tough on tender tissue, but his stomach welcomed the warmth.

"You still ain't said what you do."

"Push cattle, mostly," he lied, "a little mining, sometimes railroading . . ."

His eyes wandered about the room. It smelled flowery, a fragrance as insistent as that of the funeral parlor, overpowering but not sickening. And she smelled like it, as if her body were throwing it off and filling the four walls. Everything surrounding him seemed to emit a roseate glow, her red hair, pink skin, lips, nipples, the bedclothes, the walls, the flowered carpet, the window curtains and frilly skirt wrapped around her vanity, a soft reddish-pink hue as if wall to wall the room had captured the glow of a sunset.

"Which railroad?"

"Up in Kansas, running the line through to Topeka and Ellsworth."

"What are you doing now?"

"Nothing special . . ."

"So how do you live?" She caught herself and stared. "You ain't a criminal lawbreaker, are you? On the run . . ." She had come over to settle her charms on the edge of the bed, bracing an arm against the mattress on either side of him and leaning low to bring her face down close to his. But the sudden onset of suspicion straightened her back.

"Hell, no . . ."

"Cross your heart and hope to die?"

"You ever see this face on a wanted poster?"

"No." Down she leaned. "And that's good enough for me. Which means there ain't nothing to prevent us getting hitched."

"Brake your wheels and slow down, lady. Who said anything about getting hitched?"

"What's to stop us? We go great together." She paused and screwed up her face. "What's the matter, ain't I good enough for you? So I'm a fancy lady, so is two-thirds the women in this fine town. Hell's sweet bells, mister, I got a lot to offer besides my figger. I can cook and sew, tend bar, deal faro and blackjack, milk cows and goats, slop hogs, play the zither, you name it, I can do it. Besides which I come from church people. I'll make you one helluva wife!"

"You wouldn't like being married to me, Miss Floraday. I promise you wouldn't. I got the world's itchiest feet. You'd get so fed up packing and unpacking . . ."

She had that look in her eye he'd seen twice before, that I-see-what-I-want-and-I'm-taking-it gleam. She'd made up her mind and she wasn't about to listen to any thing he had to say intended to change it. Mercifully, a knock interrupted her.

"Mr. O'Toole?"

"Yeah?" Raider sat up.

"Somebody down in the lobby's asking to see you."

"Who?"

"She didn't give her name."

"Be right down."

Miss Floraday's blue eyes blazed. She jumped to her feet, her naked breasts bouncing like melons falling off the back of a wagon. "So you got another girl! Why, you two-timing son of a bitch!"

"It's not a girl . . ."

"He said 'she'!"

"All right, 'she.' It could be my mother, you know, or my sister."

"Or your wife, you goddamn saddletramp! Liar! Well, don't just set there with that dumb face, say something!"

"See you around."

Pulling his shirt on and thrusting the tail down into his denims, he toed into one boot, then the other, and got up. Driving his hand into his pocket, he brought out two silver dollars. "Two bucks. It's all I got on me. Is that enough?"

She snatched the money out of his hand so fast she nearly took skin with it. "Two dollars for the romp and fifty cents for the bottle!"

"For chrissakes, you drank most of it! All I got was the second swig and the last."

"You get the hell outta here and stay out, you two-timing bastard!"

Her detailed opinion of his character followed him out the door, down the narrow hallway and halfway down the stairs, to the amusement of everyone within earshot. Doc stood waiting at the bottom all smiles.

"I hope I didn't interrupt anything, Mr. O'Toole."

"I ought to smash your face in, you and your 'she'!"

"There's a message from the Wells Fargo office, from Massingale, Grater's assistant. He's come up with something and he wants to talk to us right away."

After Doc had taken his photographs and they had examined the remains of the safe and the office itself—which had been somewhat tidied, with most of the bloodstains removed before their second visit—they had interviewed the four employees. Among them had been Todd Massingale, who had since taken over as manager. At their first meeting, although eager to cooperate, Massingale had been unable to help in any way, having been at home in bed at the time of the robbery.

He was young, bright-eyed, and beardless, barely into

his twenties, but businesslike well beyond his years and experience—and visibly shaken by the tragedy. Ushering the two of them to the rear of the building, he unlocked and opened a door revealing a room stacked to the rafters with boxes and crates, a single dust-coated window locked and barred in the rear wall looking out on a barn verging on collapse.

"This is supply. We can talk privately here." Reaching into his watch pocket, he produced a small piece of yellow paper, unfolded it, and handed it to Doc.

"I found this, just a corner of it sticking out from between the floorboards. Whoever wrote it must have put it on top of the safe or on one of the tables. My guess is it got knocked to the floor and kicked aside in all the hullabaloo that followed."

Doc read the note aloud: " 'This will serve notice on Wells Fargo that no matter how big and rich you are, you can't murder an innocent boy and get away with it.' "

"No signature," said Doc folding the paper. "I'd like to keep this, Mr. Massingale."

"By all means."

"Did you say anything to the sheriff about it?"

"Not yet."

"Better keep it quiet. He's pretty much turned this case over to us."

"I won't mention it." Massingale glanced about. "This room is cramped, but like I say it's private. If you gentlemen want to talk, you're welcome to use it."

"We'd appreciate that," said Raider, taking the note from Doc and scanning it in silence. Massingale left the room, Raider closing the door behind him. He listened to his retreating steps and held up the note. "He could have planted this," he said. "I mean how come everybody, us included, passes it up and he just happens to find it?"

"Just luck? Rade, that boy doesn't strike me as the guilty party. He knows we didn't suspect him before, why should he suddenly decide to draw attention to himself? Besides, he's got to know we'd check out his relationship with Grater. From what we've been able to find out, they got along. Grater hired him and he made good . . ."

"That doesn't mean he wouldn't kill him. He wouldn't

be the first man to kill his boss so he could take his place."

"And cut off his head in the bargain? Somebody he'd worked side by side with, obviously got along with? I doubt that." Doc laced his fingers together around his knee, rocking back and forth and eying the dirty window. "No, this thing is beginning to look more and more like outside hands to me."

Raider mulled this over, his features betraying his loss of confidence in his point of view.

"I don't expect it makes any sense to search Massingale's room," he said in a dubious tone, pocketing the note. "If he's smart enough to play games with us, he sure wouldn't leave that money lying around where his landlady could find it."

"What say we shelve Mr. Massingale with the rest of the help, at least for now. Let's assume that note *is* legitimate. If so we've got ourselves a motive. We'll have to check back with the Agency and get them to check out the company."

"All five hundred offices?"

"Rade, if whoever wrote that note feels Wells Fargo is responsible for killing somebody, we've got to at least try to pinpoint what happened, and when, and who was involved."

"Express companies don't murder people."

"It could have been an accident, a baggage truck running over somebody, only his father or brother or friend doesn't see it that way and is out for revenge."

"That could be."

"Bless my soul and body! Am I to understand you're actually agreeing with me?" Doc laughed and took out a fresh Old Virginia.

"Hold off!" snapped Raider. "Don't you go lighting up that stinking hemp in here, in these close quarters. The only thing that makes me sicker than your smokes is that damn funeral parlor room. Besides, I had a couple swigs of Forty-rod up at the hotel, and I don't feel so great deep down."

"What you need is a dose of Dr. Swain's Quick Cure for Indigestion and Dyspepsia."

"Like hell I do! You already stuck me with that crap. It hits bottom and brings up the whole works!"

"It's excellent for constipation, biliousness, jaundice, sick headache, liver complaint . . ."

"I said *no!*"

"Then why don't you have a smoke along with me? That way it won't bother you . . ."

"Just hold off, damn it all!" His tone softened, his dark eyes taking on an appealing look. "Please?"

Doc hesitated, sighed, and with an air of mock martyrdom restored the twisted length of tobacco to his pocket.

They waited four days for the apple to fall while Raider did his best to stay out of Rouge Floraday's way. As he confessed to Doc, he could fight any man—"But who in hell can argue with a female?"

"Another female," observed Doc, "who else?" He had utilized his own time marking time to advantage, stocking up on supplies and fresh ingredients for his gravity batteries.

"I've got plenty of zinc, but I was getting short on copper and blue vitriol. Do you know what these Texas robbers charged me for a lousy ten pounds of vitriol? Seventy-five cents!"

"What a waste. To think you could have spent it on good liquor!"

"And wind up with a gut like yours, sure."

Word came clicking through at noon on the fourth day, casting into permanence the new complexion placed on the case by the note discovered by Massingale. Two years earlier a young expressman had been killed in a freak accident in Dayton, Ohio, his head all but torn from his body by a falling beam. The boy's older brother had taken the death extremely hard, publicly vowing to "get even" with the company for what he took to be criminal negligence. Wells Fargo had made a conscience payment of five hundred dollars, but this the brother had considered more insult than altruism, although he'd accepted it.

Information regarding the brother proved discouragingly sketchy, but it was established that Loughlin "Lock" Flanagan had been in and out of jails and territorial prison in Arizona for years before and since the younger Flanagan's death. At present Lock was thought to be running with a gang of outlaws somewhere north of the Texas border, in Indian territory.

"Lock Flanagan," said Doc. "Never heard of him."

"He's heard of you, of course," commented Raider drily. They were sitting in the wagon parked a mile out of Amarillo a hundred yards off the Randall road hooked to a line, able to transmit and receive. "His kid brother's head was crushed, so he cuts off Sam Grater's head."

"A logical form of retribution, you must admit."

"How come this Flanagan waits two whole years to get even?"

"Maybe he just got out of jail," said Doc. "It's a little hard to get even from inside, wouldn't you say?" He had his map out and was poring over it. "Indian territory," he indicated. "Rough country, No Man's Land, Comanches, Kiowa Apaches . . ."

"Flanagan wouldn't be running with Indians. Chicago said outlaws."

"Who knows?" Doc circled the area of western Oklahoma territory, aptly labeled No Man's Land, with his index finger. "What would he be doing in there? There's nothing worth the taking."

"It's good hideout territory."

Raider got down and started slowly walking across the mesquite- and snakeweed-littered ground. A Texas winter wind had come up, loosening sand and making it whirl about like ghostly dancers, a cold but far from bitter wind, nothing like the Split Cliff snow season, with its bone-aching chill and ice-covered everything.

"I know one thing," he said, turning toward the wagon where Doc still sat, his map draping his knees. "You'd be sensible to stable Judith and that wagonload of poison and get a horse between your knees."

"That's for the Agency to decide."

"Jesus Christ, Doc, can't you even get up gumption enough to suggest it?"

"Don't go getting your back up, Rade. Who knows if they'll even tell us to head north?" He folded the map and restored it to his satchel. "Who can say for certain this Flanagan is our man?"

"What do you think? I mean are you going to get real nervy for a change and maybe cook up an opinion all your own?"

"For a change, how would you like to close up your fat head?"

"How'd you like to close it up for me?"

The receiver came to life. Doc waved the oncoming Raider back and listened, his eyes enlarging in their sockets, a pathetic groan escaping his throat.

"Oh boy, oh boy, oh boy . . ." Tapping out acknowledgment with one hand, he stilled Raider with the other. "There's been a second murder and robbery."

"Indian territory?"

"Down the way, southeast, Wichita Falls."

"What do you mean, 'down the way'? That's better than two hundred miles!"

The receiver resumed clicking. The body of the manager of the Wells Fargo office in Wichita Falls had been discovered hours earlier lying beside his emptied safe, the head conspicuously absent.

Missing as well was $108,000.

5

The bomb that had been dropped into Doc's lap and was speedily bouncing into Raider's posed an immediate problem to the two operatives. To head toward Wichita Falls would mean abandoning the search for Lock Flanagan even before starting it.

Raider insisted, cajoled, demanded, threatened bodily injury, and finally induced Doc to transmit a request to the Chicago office for permission for the pair to split up. Doc would head southeast for Wichita Falls to investigate the new murder-robbery while Raider rode north into Indian territory. "God's land, but No Man's," as those passing through described it.

It was agreed that Amarillo would serve as their temporary command post; any message one might have for the other would be dispatched to the Western Union office there. The messages would employ a basic code.

"It's very simple, Rade."

"You've got to remember I only got as far as the seventh grade."

They sat in their hotel room in the Amarillo House, a bottle of Forty-rod and two cracked tumblers on the table between them, Doc sitting with his sleeves rolled up, his derby tilted high on the back of his head, pencil and paper in hand, his cup of kindness brimming over with patience for his somewhat less mentally proficient coworker.

A rat scraped its way through the interior of the wall at Raider's back; a gun went off in the saloon across the street. Doc sighed, got up, shut the window to muffle the distractions in the street below, locked the door, and sat. Placing the six-point green silk shaded lamp between them directly over the blank piece of paper, he motioned Raider closer.

"We'll use Julius Caesar," he said quietly.

"Do something else this time. Julius Caesar is too simple; any idiot can figure it out."

"Which means there's no chance you'll be confused." Raider snorted, glared, reached for his half-filled tumbler of whiskey, and sipped.

"Just hear me out," continued Doc. "This time around we'll give it a slight variation. Instead of making the interval plus three, we'll make it plus three for the first exchange, plus six for the second."

"Plus nine for the third."

"Right. Then if there's a fourth exchange, we'll go back to three. So in my first message to you and yours to me, A becomes D, B becomes E and so on."

Raider yawned his boredom fully into his partner's face. "The second time A becomes G, B becomes H . . ."

"Right. And plus nine the third time. Okay, I'll do a plus nine, you decode." Doc took up his pencil and wrote:

ANCDA WRWPC XJCON OXDAC Q

Raider took the pencil from Doc, turned the paper around, and slowly and laboriously decoded, licking the tip of the pencil after each individual letter, getting his fill of the taste of graphite by the time he was done and washing it off his tongue with drink. He turned the paper back around with his free hand for Doc's appraisal.

Doc read: " 'Returning to A the fourth.' Right. Interval plus three, plus six, plus nine."

"Then back to interval plus three. Okay. I just hope no sharp-eyed telegrapher with nefarious ideas breaks it. For chrissakes, a four-year-old with one eye and half his brain could figure out Julius Caesar, even with changing intervals!"

"I just wanted to make it as easy as possible for you, Rade."

"You're funny."

They parted company the next morning, Judith loping away dragging Doc's dilapidated little wagon toward Claude, then Goodnight, and eventually Wichita Falls while Raider rode in a northeasterly direction in the hope of picking up Lock Flanagan's trail.

They had shared breakfast, shortly after arising, at a

greasy spoon down the street from the hotel. It boasted far more cockroaches than customers and the flies outnumbered the crawlers in attendance by twenty to one. Fifty cents cash laid on the sticky table had fetched cold and greasy overfried eggs with the consistency of rotten poncho rubber, charred toast, and coffee strong enough to float Doc's gold tooth in. But the meal was warming and filling and something to do together before saying goodbye.

Raider rode out of town at a gallop, but slowed the bay and threw a glance back over his shoulder at his partner's wagon heading in the opposite direction, Judith's feed bucket swinging from its hook on the tailgate, the cloth bonnet shuddering under its supports as the homely contraption's wheels found every rut lacing the well-traveled road.

Raider sighed. He'd miss the dandified son of a bitch, that gleaming crockery grin of his, his big words, slick tongue, annoying determination to follow up every damn case assigned by the Chicago office strictly by the book, snapping pictures with his Primo camera of everything from busted jaws, windows, and safe doors to dead men's dicks and dentures. And in-between times foisting off everything from nerve and brain pills to arnicated carbolic salve on every gullible sodbuster, hell-raiser, and bean-brained whore west of the Mississippi.

God, but the bastard could needle! Prick a man purple with rage, slipping it into the soft and tender parts of his ego and his pride. Insulting? Sweet Jesus . . . How he had gotten this far through life without somebody taking a five-pound Kelly Axe to his head was a miracle on a par with Moses parting the Red Sea. The most outrageous, most downright discouraging aspect of the whole dismal experience was that with all his infuriatingly bad-to-miserable traits and habits, you couldn't help liking the guy. Maybe because under all the sham and show and shine he boasted the balls of a bull and a coolness any Indian would tip his braids to.

And examining him, that was Doc's strong suit, the sham, the show, the shine. He looked anything but a good man with a gun. Nothing in his appearance suggested toughness, resiliance, resourcefulness. Just the opposite, actually. But how many times had Raider seen him face down a bad customer who would hit the ground with a bullet in his brisket and a look on his face that said he couldn't believe it had happened, couldn't conceive of his being taken down by somebody so soft-looking and so dudishly dressed.

Doc had come West from Eastern money. His father had run a banking house in New York, but Doc had found loans and interest rates and the other trappings of high finance dull. He had taken it as long as he could, then exchanged his desk for a job as a detective with the New York Central Railroad. On a trip east, Wagner had talked with him at length, was impressed, and brought him to Chicago to introduce him to Allan Pinkerton.

Raider's background couldn't have been more diametrically opposed to his partner's if a dime novelist had devised it for him. After his father had died, he'd sold the family farm near Viola, Fulton County, Arkansas, and had wandered around admittedly trying to find himself. He had drifted to Sioux City and had chanced to hear Allan Pinkerton speak at a fund-raising rally for the local police. Pinkerton's ideas on lawlessness and how to deal with it had impressed him. He had approached him later and talked with him briefly, had been given a card, and two weeks later found himself sitting in the same chair in the boss's office in the Agency in Chicago that Doc had sat in three days earlier. He was interviewed, his background, like Doc's, investigated. And he was hired.

Neither man had been old enough to fight in the war, both barely sixteen by the time it was over. This shortage of years, however, in no way discouraged them from taking sides and battling over the issues that had separated the Union whenever they were at a loss for something to argue about. A rare occurrence.

Enough of reminiscences. It was getting to be time to be thinking about the present, about himself and the job ahead. His destination lay across the Texas Panhandle, a finger of land no more than 50 miles wide and 160 long, a misshapen, oversized crater nestled within the borders of Kansas, Colorado, New Mexico, and Texas and the one-hundredth meridian, which marked the western territorial limit of the Oklahoma lands assigned to the Indians.

This led inevitably to No Man's Land becoming a

highly popular retreat for people operating illegally, it being outside the jurisdiction of either red or white administration.

Raider carried a .44 Remington holstered onto a forty-loop Anson Mills belt and Haber Selkirk's Winchester snug in his rifle boot. Acutely mindful of the reputation of No Man's Land, and the citizenry infesting it, he had no doubt that his arsenal would come in handy. Finding the proverbial needle in the haystack would likely be easier than finding Lock Flanagan in No Man's Land, if indeed he was hiding out there.

The weather turned colder the further north he ventured. The Canadian River was frozen over, the bay skittering across the creaking blue ice fringed with old snow along both banks like mile-long rabbit pelts pressed into place for warmth. The wind slapped at Raider's bare cheeks, deepening their natural ruddiness, obliging him to mask his features with his bandanna.

No Man's Land. Jesus, if he didn't pull the neck of the chicken out of the pot every goddamn time! While Doc always seemed to come up with a meaty thigh or a chunk of breast. Ten times out of ten! In five days he would be sitting in a whorehouse in Wichita Falls surrounded by buxom bitches likely drawing straws to see which would get first crack at his meat. Sitting in a plush, overstuffed gent's easy chair, feet up, drinking goblets full of that fancy frog wine he was so fond of, gold-toothpicking his smile, relaxing, enjoying the time of his misbegotten, luck-lined life.

The son of a bitch!

The bay was fighting for breath as it climbed the opposite bank, blowing vapor from its nostrils like a Rocky Mountain locomotive struggling up a steep grade. Raider dismounted, collected an armful of sticks, and led the horse to a nearby buffalo wallow, its bottom strewn with chips. Down on his haunches he got a fire started, then fetched the horse down into the wallow out of the wind and into the warmth. He fed it oats and a hat half-filled with water, then made coffee for himself. He had packed very little, figuring that with any luck the weather would hold cold but snowless, and he'd be reaching Boise City in the Cimmaron across Coldwater Creek and the North Canadian some ninety miles up the line in a couple of days. Boise City would be the first and undoubtedly the only point for a hundred miles in every direction from which he'd be able to wire Amarillo.

Not that he expected to have any news of Flanagan by then.

A mischievous gust of wind curled down the wall of the wallow, slapped the fire, and killed it. *Fuck it,* thought Raider. He should be making tracks anyway, not killing valuable daylight time talking to his horse and himself and sipping watery coffee. Scattering the ashes, he collected a saddlebag full of chips for future fires and, mounting up, resumed the northward trek. In his offside saddlebag he had stuffed a full bottle of Forty-rod before departing from Amarillo. Lifting his leg and unstrapping the bag, he brought out the bottle. It was icy cold even through his glove. Uncorking it with his teeth, he downed a gulp and a second, then restored the cork and the bottle to the bag.

He continued on through the desolate bunch-grass-studded land passing soddies and ramshackle barns, deserted spreads, the owners surrendering to the elements that made No Man's Land so suitable a name. People had come from Kansas and Colorado, from Texas and eastern Oklahoma, to challenge this slip whose very existence and solitary purpose seemed to be to test the extremes of God's weather. In a way the area was as seductive as a beautiful women carrying a stone in the cavity customarily reserved for the heart. In the spring or early summer, lovely green grass resplendent with wild flowers in abundance carpeted the sweeping prairies. Buffalo and deer grazed on the succulent grama and bluestem blades. Purling streams and deep, swift rivers of the sweetest-tasting water in the West further beautified the land.

But come late July and August, and the green prairies thirsting for rain surrendered their lush loveliness to a lifeless brown, the land becoming parched and overspread with death—to plants, to creatures, to men and their families. The blazing sun broiled and baked the landscape. Burning winds helped to wither the grass and trees, smothering crops and cattle under layers of dust.

Those who stuck it out clinging to hope and faith in eventual deliverance perished of the heat and thirst and starvation, their passing celebrated by whirling winds, spiraling wraiths dancing against the round, red eye of the sun.

In time winter arrived, clutching the land, the bitter, bone-binding cold bringing blizzards sweeping across the prairies.

Winter . . . Into the teeth of it Raider rode.

6

Doc never seemed to tire of reminding his partner that the Allan Pinkerton Detective Agency was the most businesslike business in the continental United States, its investigative efforts as painstakingly planned and doggedly carried through to completion as the spinning of a spider's web. Mindful of this, Raider had little doubt but that an artist's sketch of Lock Flanagan would be waiting for him in Boise City.

He reached there without incident, stabled his horse, feasted on steak and potatoes, and picked up the sketch of Lock Flanagan at the Western Union office. Flanagan's face was that of a hunted, haunted man, the eyes wary, all but shifting from side to side across the paper. His nose had been broken halfway down to his flaring nostrils, healing itself with a telltale bump. His jaw was so square it resembled half a building brick thrust into position under his thin-lipped mouth. It was a face Raider could have easily spotted a hundred yards away through a driving rain. What disturbed him, however, was not the man's looks, but his physical dimensions, the most noteworthy carefully detailed on the back of the paper. Flanagan was reputed to be six-foot-seven, with shoulders "half the width of a double ox yoke" and hands capable of providing suitable substitutes for eight-pound sledgehammers. Added to this intelligence was the comment that Raider's quarry had an inordinate fondness for breaking the bones of people who crossed him, a tendency undoubtedly traceable to his Irish ancestry and the violent temper customarily associated with individuals of such origin.

No slouch himself at working with fists, elbows, knees, and boots at close quarters, carrying 185 sinewy pounds on his six-foot-two-inch frame, Raider nevertheless had little liking for physical mixing with people who outweighed him by forty pounds and outreached him three inches or more. He had experienced no small number of encounters with such specimens and had invariably emerged from these frays aching, broken, and pessimistic about the odds against eventual full recovery.

On Christmas Day, while Boise City's Methodist church bells rang out melodious accompaniment to roving bands of carolers, Raider reluctantly reined his own holiday spirits and left town with Merry Christmases assailing him on all sides. He traveled under a leaden sky threatening to split and lower enough snow to effectively bury the world of western Oklahoma. He was crossing the border into Beaver County when the blizzard struck, the wind catching it descending and whipping it furiously.

An hour earlier he had stopped by Elation to load up on canned beans, biscuit, and other delicacies of the trail and to thaw the remaining contents of his canteen. Refilling it, he took the precaution of stuffing it inside his jacket to keep the water from freezing with the heat of his steak-filled stomach.

As the day drew to its close and the storm continued to rage, he stopped a second time at a sod house, the owner permitting him to stall the bay in the barn and offering him space in a room already occupied by three other travelers. Four men would be sharing two beds. A far cry from the Amarillo House, concluded Raider dejectedly, but better than tucking a snowdrift under his chin.

"Titus Z. Campbell's the name," said the round-shouldered, hook-nosed, tic-tormented owner of the soddy, extending his hand and grasping Raider's.

"Walter O'Toole," said Raider. "Pleased to meet you."

"Your mount'll be okay in the barn. I built her with my own two hands. She's sturdy as stone. We be a mite short on grub. I warn't expectin' four o' you to show up all in the space of a hour. Doggone weather hit so fast, though, I guess you and the three in the other room just took one look at the sky and come runnin' for the first chimbley in sight."

"You bet *I* did."

The house was typical of the territory, constructed of rectangles of sod. It was approximately fourteen by thirty-six feet, with a ten-by-twelve L-shaped addition at one end that served as the guest room. The rafters, mostly unadzed tree trunks, reached from the walls to a heavy log ridgepole. Willow brush had been laid on the roof and flattened to form a solid matting, a base for a layer of sod that was carefully mortared with clay.

The windows were barely a foot square, most of them

covered with burlap, glass being almost impossible to come by in the area and harder to preserve once installed when hailstones the size of hens' eggs came flying down from Kansas.

With the door closed against the storm, the only light came from two kerosene lamps set at either end of a table filled with jugs of home-squeezed corn liquor, bringing back to Raider's mind old man Crowder's "squeezin's pizen, fifty cents the jug," which the Selkirks had thrived on in quantity.

An Acme air-tight heating stove stood in the center of the room glowing fiercely. The chimney top had evidently piled over with snow, and little or no smoke was escaping, most of it sneaking out the edges of the stove door and around the pipe joint, the collar, and damper handle. It was gradually filling the room, creating a resemblance to an opium den. Straight- and round-backed chairs and three-legged stools comprised most of the remaining furniture, while a double shelf suspended from the far wall displayed flower-patterned china plates in various sizes providing solitary evidence of feminine influence.

Titus Z. spied Raider looking at the shelf and read his thoughts.

"My old lady passed on about a year back. The consumption. I buried her in the barn. It was her last wish. How's about a snort? Fresh-squeezed, make it myself."

Titus Z. Campbell's corn liquor tasted like corn liquor, but with something nauseating added, slight to the taste, but undeniably present. Likely a mouse had crawled down the neck of the jug offered him by the old man—and having drunk its fill, drowned. The soddy abounded with vermin, everything alive bent on escaping the storm.

"Sounds like that wind's bent on turning this place around so's the front door faces north," observed Titus Z. with a chuckle. His attempt at humor was only a disguise for his nervousness. The tics under his watery gray eyes jumped both alternately and in unison. "Bring your jug and come on into the guest room. Meet the fellas."

Titus Z.'s three guests sat on one of the two beds playing three-handed stud for matches by the feeble glow of a candle, the snipped-off end of an empty bean can serving as its holder. The two windows in the cramped little room were covered with burlap nailed down at all four corners but threatening to tear loose at any moment, so powerful and persistent was the wind attacking the house.

The stench of unwashed bodies was so strong Raider was surprised that the candle was able to remain upright. On entering the room he decided on the spot that not one of the three men had bathed since water was invented and wouldn't have recognized a bar of sulfur soap from a brick of cut loaf sugar candy. The three were introduced to Walter O'Toole as Jeb, Simon, and Vic, last names mentioned but just as speedily forgotten. Raider had made a lifelong practice of committing first names only to memory when it came to multiple introductions, particularly when he knew he'd probably never again lay eyes on those to whom he was being introduced. He was invited to join the stud game but declined, returning instead to the living room and sitting with Titus Z. and discussing the weather.

An hour later, after feasting on his own beans warmed on top of the stove and washing them down with corn, he slogged through the snow to the barn to see to the bay, returned, and positioned his wet boots upside down against the stove legs. He then retired for the night, stretching his weary length beside Vic already out and snoring, bellowing louder than a mortally wounded steer.

The wind continued to buffet the soddy, slapping at the burlap window covers, sneaking in and stirring the smoke-filled air.

Raider dropped off around midnight, but he was not asleep more than an hour before a loud crash awoke him, sitting him straight up in bed. The burlap rags covering both windows had torn loose and snow had piled into the room, forming rapidly growing drifts at the feet of both beds. But it was the noise awakening him that commanded his immediate attention, that and the mournful lowing of cattle in distress. Glancing out the window, the gale whipping his face, he saw what had happened. Range cattle driven by the blizzard had climbed onto the barn roof and caved it in. Rousing the others, Raider ran into the other room, hauled his boots on, pulled on his jacket, hat, and gloves, and raced for the barn.

The bay and the others' horses were shaken and as nervous as cats up a tree, but had escaped injury. The cattle were less fortunate. Two steers had broken their necks and were dying, and a number of others dragged about on broken legs. Titus Z. brought both lamps from the corn jug table into the barn and, taking stock of the situation, began cussing like a muleskinner.

Raider and the others left him to deal with the problem, bringing their horses into the house. At Titus Z.'s insistence two were stabled in the little bedroom, leaving scarcely enough room for a half-grown rat to maneuver in. The snow clogging the chimney stack was removed, the snow on the bedroom floor was shoveled out, the burlap window covers were replaced, double-nailed at the corners, and everybody went back to bed leaving the invading cattle to wander on their way.

Raider woke the next morning to the sight of Vic sitting up in bed intently studying the sketch of Lock Flanagan. Raider snatched it from his grasp, folded it, and jammed it back into his pocket.

"I was just lookin', mister."

"Try minding your own fucking business and keeping your stinking hands off other people's property!" snapped Raider irritably.

Vic bristled, licking his fat lips, made fists, swung his feet to the floor, and readied himself for combat.

"You got a big mouth, O'Toole. How'd you like me to bloody it shut for ya?"

Raider was sitting on the edge of the bed. Without his even raising his eyes to the target, up came his right, catching Vic flush on the jaw and toppling him between the two horses with a crash that startled both beasts, shook the room, and woke up Jeb and Simon. They blinked, rubbed their eyes, and stared at Vic stretched out under his mare.

"What hit him?" Simon asked.

"His horse kicked him," said Raider. He arose, got ready, paid Titus Z. twenty-five cents for the bed and fifty for the jug, got out, and ten minutes later was urging the bay eastward into the washed-out white eye of the rising sun. Head down, he searched unsuccessfully for the road. During the night the temperature had dropped low enough to break the ball, but daylight was gradually lifting it. The wind had died, but before doing so had erected drifts twenty feet high and higher.

The disastrous consequences of the blizzard were scarcely restricted to the collapse of Titus Z.'s barn and the loss of nearly half his neighbor's wandering herd. Raider had seen the misbehavior of many a blizzard in his time. The wind roaring down from the north carrying this much snow had probably delivered it in quantity as far south as Waco. Thousands of head of cattle had to have been lost, hundreds of families snowbound, many facing starvation, and a blanket of destruction thrown over the entire Southern Plains.

Heading north, crossing the frozen Beaver Creek, the bay picking its way skillfully down long avenues blown clear between drifts, Raider wondered how Doc had come through the storm. Wichita Falls lay nearly 250 miles southeast of his own present position. No sod houses there; logs, clapboarding, and stone served as construction materials for the ranch and farmhouses and town buildings of Wichita Falls and adjacent areas. Windows boasted glass; barns were built to last; there was no shortage of shovels and plows and the muscle required to use them.

Not that the Doc Weatherbee Raider knew would be out in company with the good citizens clearing the streets and pathways. Not in a thousand years. Manual labor—sweating, lifting, straining—was not Doc's preference . . . not unless somebody in authority came after him with a club or whip and forced him into it. Blizzard or no, drifts twenty, fifty, sixty feet high, Raider would bet his last hard dollar that right at the moment his partner was sitting on the edge of the bed of the prettiest whore in town in a cozy hotel room, regaling her with tales of his manly prowess, killing time between sexual bouts while awaiting restoration of the seminal juices necessary to resume activities.

The son of a bitch!

As if mental pictures of Doc romping with some curvaceous beauty naked as a newborn jay weren't disturbing enough, even more irritating was the problem currently occupying Raider's lap. Finding Lock Flanagan in No Man's Land under these conditions was promising to be about as easy as finding love in a morgue.

7

Raider's runaway imagination notwithstanding, Doc had not hit it quite as lucky as his partner thought. The northernbound half of the team greatly overrated Judith's rate of progress in the direction of Wichita Falls. By the time the storm that had hit the soddy reached man and mule and wagon, the combination had gotten only as far as Tell on the western border of Childress County. There, at the bar of a saloon displaying above its bat-wing doors the ingenious name "Tells All—Finest Liquor, Cleanest Glasses West of Philadelphia," over a bottle of St. Louis scotch, Doc made the acquaintance of a buxom young blonde calling herself Heather DeWinter. Jokes about the blizzard and the lady's name helped to cement a firm association that quickly blossomed into friendship in an iron-spring bed on a double-thick feather mattress where Heather went to work on Doc with a vigor and tenacity roughly comparable to the attack of a famished tigress upon a helpless goat.

Bringing his tool to a hardness hardly surpassed by that of the iron bed frame, she inserted it full length between her jaws and proceeded to wallop the living hell out of it with her tongue. So incredibly hard, so tenaciously did she suck, that Doc had fleeting visions of both his balls hurtling up his cock, one after the other.

"Easy, easy, easy, dear heart."

Heather ignored his plea, sucking him dry, mercifully leaving both testicles intact, but reducing his cock to a pale limp lump resembling a deflated penny balloon.

Glancing down at it resting upon his balls, he decided that as long as it hung between his legs it would never be hard again.

He was wrong. Down on her pink knees, firmly gripping his legs, she turned her hot, wet mouth loose on the lump a second time, miraculously restoring its spikelike solidity,

52

refilling his balls, and readying him for a second excursion into ecstasy.

"Want to fuck me?" she squealed, her baby blue eyes dancing merrily.

"Ahhhh . . ."

Before he could complete his response, she had pushed him down onto the bed and was mounting his cock with the suddenness and agility of a rodeo rider overlegging a wild mustang. The drab little room, with its framed watercolors of birds, beasts, rippling creeks, and jagged peaks, swam before his eyes as she thrust her cunt down upon his manhood and began wrenching away at it, all but jerking it free of its mooring.

"Easy, easy . . ."

She bounced and twisted and angled her body, driving his head into every nook and cranny of her box. Then, to his astonishment, she suddenly stopped bouncing, twisting, thrusting, and angling and began spinning slowly around, turning her entire body, using his captive cock as a pivot. Visions of it corkscrewing into a permanent spiral flashed across his mind. Up came his hands to stop her, but she brushed past them, continuing to revolve.

The worst was yet to come. He came, not a natural ejaculation so cleverly devised by nature, so gratifyingly experienced; instead his semen forced its way upward through the spiral conduit. His balls driving their load against the restricting pressure felt as if twin hammers were striking them. Noting the agony in his eyes, she twisted in the opposite direction, straightening his cock permitting his load comfortable, painless escape, relieving the agonizing pressure building below.

Draining him, she jumped off, all but taking his manhood with her and causing him to yell loudly.

"Jesus Christ, lady, where in hell did you ever learn to diddle like that?"

"My fourth husband. He loves it."

"You mean you're married?"

"Nope. Want to get married?"

"Ahh . . . what do you say to a drink?"

Heather could suck and Heather could fuck and Heather could drink. Like a horse rescued from Death Valley.

"I'm what they call an alcoholic," she confessed as she

polished off the last quarter of the bottle in three generous gulps. "I drink like a fish."

"You drink like a whale."

"I just got to have booze."

Doc shook his head. "How old are you, Heather?"

"Twenty-two going on twenty-three."

"That's bad."

"You saying I'm too old for you?"

"I'm saying you're too young to be an alcoholic. How would you like to cure it?"

"Could you, Doc? Really?"

Getting up, gingerly caressing his genitals and relieved at the absence of blood, he reached for his trousers with the other hand.

"Come on down to the stable with me. I've got just the thing for you."

Out shot her hand grabbing his cock.

"No, no, dammit! I'm talking about medicine. You take it, I mean faithfully for one solid month, and you'll never drink another drop of liquor as long as you live."

"Honest?"

"Cross my heart. Let's go, get your clothes and coat and galoshes on."

"All I need is my coat and galoshes."

8

In line with Doc's explicit instructions, Judith was being given the best possible care, wearing a pure gum rubber horse blanket over her plaid traveling blanket, feasting on clean oats, imbibing fresh water, and enjoying hay of a quality comparable to that reserved for the nest of a champion egg layer.

Heather waited while Doc rummaged through his wagon, uncovered a large unopened wooden box, the top nailed shut, and set it on the seat.

"This place smells like horse manure," commented Heather, sniffing and glancing about the stable.

"That it does," said Doc, inwardly marveling at her perceptivity and wondering, not for the first time, if dumbness was an intrinsic trait or an acquired one. Getting a claw hammer out of his toolbox, he opened one of the cover boards and produced a rectangular-shaped paper-covered box displaying a hairless and somewhat distressed-looking individual upending a bottle of unlabeled rotgut and downing its contents. Alongside the poor afflicted gentleman printed in stark black block letters were the words:

STOP DRINKING!

German Liquor Cure

Guaranteed to destroy all desire for liquor.
Results unconditionally guaranteed.
Used successfully by 4 million Germans.

"I'm not German," said Heather sadly.

"Makes no difference."

Unlocking the end paper tab, Doc reached inside and removed the bottle. Wound around it was a pamphlet printed in three languages, including English. In brief, the German Liquor Cure promised that if a single teaspoon of the cure was imbibed three times daily before each meal, within thirty days all desire for liquor would vanish.

Along with curing alcoholism, the cure guaranteed to improve the appetite and the digestion. And regulate the bowels.

"I'm going to give you four bottles. Ninety-six doses, enough for thirty-two straight days," said Doc, piling the boxes into her hands. "But you've got to promise to take your doses three times every day. You can't miss one, not one."

"Not one. How does it taste?"

"Try it."

Uncorking the bottle inside the opened package, she downed a healthy gulp.

"Wait, wait," gasped Doc. "Taste it, don't empty the whole damned bottle. It's not booze, dear heart, it's medicine."

"It tastes delicious."

"There's a little orange flavoring in it." Doc covered the four packages in her hands with his hands. "Three teaspoonfuls a day every day. You'll be on your own, I'm pulling out for New Orleans first thing tomorrow," he lied.

"For thirty days, before meals. I understand. I'll do it, cross my heart!"

"In a month you won't be able to stand the sight of liquor." He tapped the pasteboard boxes in her hands. "If it can do it for four million Germans, it can do it for Heather DeWinter."

Judith snorted and stamped one hoof as if, having heard Doc's sales pitch, she was announcing her skepticism.

The north wind that had brought the blizzard and the widespread devastation had died when it stopped snowing. Early the next morning, however, it came to life with the sun and began sweeping away great patches, leveling drifts, opening the way down to Kirkland for Judith and Doc. A little over a hundred miles separated them from Wichita Falls, a day's ride for a man on horseback, but Judith was no horse and would require better than two days, burdened as she was with the crate-filled wagon.

Doc was at the stable at seven o'clock, seeing to Judith's breakfast, backing her into the shafts, double-checking her single-breasted harness, traces, and belly band, and checking the wheel-greasing job done by the stableman the night before. He paid his bill and left town by way of the Kirkland road. The wind had done its job well, as if in atonement for the havoc it had helped to wreak the previous night. Vast stretches of land, devoted with the coming of spring to wheat and cotton, now blanketed with winter's white, creating a vista that filled him with a lonely feeling, and a vague twitching in his loins recalled memory of Heather DeWinter and her talents.

He had not charged her the usual two-dollar retail fee for the four bottles of German Liquor Cure, feeling in fairness that the services she had provided him more than offset in value his wholesale cost of the cure.

He would miss Heather DeWinter, the drab little room with its homely watercolors, the iron bed that clanked at climax, the Tells All Saloon; but that was the nature of the row he had chosen to hoe. Pinkerton operatives kept moving. Another decapitated body, directly connected, he hoped, with Sam Grater's murder, both crimes traceable to Lock Flanagan, and one more case journal would soon be closing. If, that is, Raider succeeded in finding Flanagan and bringing him in.

There was nothing overly complicated about the case; the only hard part, actually, was Raider's assignment. No Man's Land must have caught the full force of the storm, thought Doc. Even in fair weather that most notorious neck of northern Oklahoma was no place to wander. The resident Kiowa Apaches and Comanches had little affection for each other, but considerably less for Pale-eyes. Not that Raider couldn't handle himself—hand to hand, using a gun, a knife, almost anything in reach. Once in a shootout with two mail-pouch thieves in a woods a half day's ride north of Topeka, by the most remarkable coincidence conceivable, all four combatants had run out of ammunition at the same time. Doc had looked on in amazement as Raider had picked up a passing skunk by the muzzle, heaving it over the rock the two thieves were hiding behind. One after the other came flying over, landing on their butts, hands in the air. The skunk had vented its ire and its anal secretion against the rock. Holding empty guns on the two men, Raider and Doc had marched them to town and into a cell. Case closed.

Doc would never forget Raider's response to his, Doc's, comment on his quick thinking:

"One thing's sure, that move sure wasn't in Allan Pinkerton's General Principles."

It was this attitude, and Doc's persisting failure to anticipate Raider's next move in practically every case that made partnership with the man so fascinating. Doc had never met anybody so gifted with the talent for pulling the unexpected. Not having Raider around to needle and send scooting up telegraph poles to hook the wire to in sub-zero weather, talking to Judith instead of arguing with Raider, kidding him mercilessly, to the point—on more than one occasion—when words had failed Raider and he'd substituted his fists, all these things combined to make every day minus his presence as dull as a sermon delivered too loudly to sleep through.

Slipping off one genuine imported peccary hogskin glove, Doc inserted his thumb and forefinger into his mouth and removed his gold molar, a birthday gift from Raider to replace the real tooth dislodged by Raider's left in a fit of pique. Studying the tooth with the warmth of affection rising behind his vest, Doc then snapped it back into place, grit his teeth to secure it, replaced his glove, flipped the reins over Judith's flanks, and speeded her up.

"I miss that old boy, Judith. He's more fun than any man I know and the best part of all is he doesn't even realize it."

A muffled giggle sounded behind Doc's back. A loud hush . . . another giggle, a gurgling sound . . .

"Whoa, girl." Winding the reins around the brake handle, Doc swiveled about, pulled the cloth bonnet open, and looked inside. There seated on crates were three women: two strangers and Heather DeWinter.

" 'Lo, Doc," mumbled Heather in a slurring tone, slowly lifting her hand and waggling her fingers in greeting. "Thish ish Mabel and Fern. We're comin' wish you to Nor . . . Nor . . . Nor .. ."

"New Orleans," interjected Mabel, like Heather a blonde but with longer hair in a lighter, almost platinum shade. Fern was a brunette, small and doe-eyed, with breasts that looked, from under her ermine-trimmed jacket, to be three sizes too large for her chest.

"What in hell——" began Doc. Ducking his head, holding his derby in place with one hand, he climbed back inside.

Heather endeavored to explain, but she was too far gone to put coherence let alone common sense into the attempt. Spying the crate containing the German Liquor Cure broken into and all but emptied of its contents, with small corkless brown bottles and their pasteboard cartons scattered about the floor, he concluded on the spot that Heather's condition had not been induced by alcohol.

Ostensibly she had managed to get as high as a silo dome on the cure. No catfish had ever been more securely hooked. Her eyes refused to focus, her pretty face teetered from side to side, her mouth hung open ridiculously. As his eyes traveled southward down her body, she suddenly doubled over, falling across the crate, her face finding his feet, giggling hysterically. Grabbing her by the arms, Fern and Mabel pulled her back up to a sitting position and held her there.

"German likker cur. . . . 'Lishus, besh tashtin' likker cur ever made. S'help me, Gawd." With this Heather fell backward, encountering a stack of homeopathic medicines in cardboard cartons set in wooden-edged frames. She began snoring loudly.

"What in hell do you think you're up to, stowing away in my wagon?" snapped Doc angrily. "You've got one helluva nerve. . . ."

"It was Heather's idea," said Fern batting her eyes innocently. "We decided to leave Tell."

"So why didn't you take the damn stage?"

"We've only got two dollars between the three of us," Mabel explained.

"Two dollars? Chrissakes, you could earn ten times that among the three of you in four hours!" He could feel the anger rising in his cheeks. The sight of Heather snoring away peacefully, contentment capturing her features, and the other two sitting there as comfortably as if they were awaiting patrons in a brothel parlor was rapidly churning his gut to the point of explosion.

"If you didn't blow every damn dollar that comes

into your hands you wouldn't be broke! Did that ever oc-
cur to you?"

"What are you so upset about?" Fern asked. "We're
only hitching a ride. We haven't stolen anything."

"Lady, that goddamn case of liquor cure held seventy-
two goddamn bottles. There's no more than eight or ten
left. Your friend there has swallowed goddamn near
thirty bucks' worth of merchandise! If that isn't stealing,
I'd like to know what is. On your feet, the two of you.
Get her up!"

"She's sleeping," began Mabel.

"I don't give a good gaddamn if she's stone cold dead.
Up and get out, all three of you. The party's over!"

"We'd be willing to earn our way to New Orleans,"
said Mabel smiling seductively and running her hands
fetchingly up the insides of her thighs.

"No thanks."

"You're not going to turn us out onto the road and
make us walk!" Fern put on a hurt look. "It's freezing out
there. And we'd have to carry Heather. . . ."

"You can roll her into a snowball and push her to
Kirkland!"

"Please . . ."

"Have a heart," said Mabel in a little-girl voice.
"Heather says you have a heart of gold."

Heather continued snoring without letup, licking her lips
hungrily, ostensibly thirsting for her next bottle of the
cure.

"Heather says you're a marvelous person," said Fern.

"Heather doesn't say a goddamn thing. All she does is
empty my bottles into her goddamn face! Christ, she's
lucky she didn't break into my Brandreth Liquid Cathar-
tic supply by mistake!" He threw up his hands. "Can
you imagine what this place would look like about now?"
He sighed and, placing his hands against his cheeks,
groaned audibly. "Okay, okay, okay, I'll take you as far
as Kirkland. . . ."

"Why not New Orleans?" inquired Fern.

"I've got important business there," he lied. "And it
doesn't include you three."

Heather snored on.

"If you let us travel with you, we'll give you half of all

we take in," suggested Mabel. "We can open up our own little house on Bourbon Street. . . ."

"That's not the kind of business I had in mind. Kirkland it is, take it or leave it."

"You can drop the two of us," said Fern, "but you'll have a hard time getting rid of Heather."

Mabel nodded. "Mister, that little girl is in love with you."

"She's in love with my German Liquor Cure. Cut the conversation. Wake her up by the time we get to Kirkland and tell her the plan. We'll be getting there in about ten minutes."

"It shouldn't take more than a week to get to New Orleans," said Mabel, abandoning her appealing little-girl tone and glaring at him frigidly.

"You'll see," added Fern. "You'll be grateful for the company, won't he, Mabe?"

"You bet."

"For the last time, you're all three getting out in Kirkland if I have to boot you over the tailgate!"

Mabel laughed mirthlessly. "You try, sucker, and we'll yell bloody murder."

"We'll swear you kidnapped us from a young ladies' finishing school in Kansas City or someplace," Fern added. "It'll be our word against yours, three against one."

"Two against two, flat-ass!" snapped Doc. "Your friend on the floor there won't go along with it."

Both girls laughed uproariously. "Sucker, it was her idea!" burst Fern.

Mabel reached out and patted Doc on the cheek. "You be a good boy, get up front and get your mule moving and everything'll work out just fine."

Heather snored on, still smiling, almost—Doc assured himself—slightly nodding agreement with her two friends.

Goddamn bitches! If Wagner in Chicago ever got wind of this one, he'd have Doc's ass in a sling from the highest limb of the nearest cottonwood tree! If there was one thing Allan Pinkerton was stone cold dead against it was conduct unbecoming an operative, particularly when said man was actively involved in a case.

Mabel was right. If he tried to kick the three of them out in Kirkland, they would yell the damn roof off the town. If he wasn't careful, he could wind up behind bars with their lies holding him there for a damn trial. Christ, he'd never get to Wichita Falls! He'd never get a chance to begin investigating. . . .

His Diamondback pistol lay with his telegraph equipment under the floorboards in its specially constructed box. If he went about it cleverly, he might, he supposed, haul it out and wave the three of them out of his life before Judith came within sight of Kirkland.

But no, there was a better, surer way of getting rid of them.

"Okay," he said in the voice of weary resignation. "I'll take you to New Orleans."

"Now you're making sense," said Mabel.

"On one condition . . ."

"No conditions," said Fern. "Just get up front and get to driving."

"One condition. When we get there we split up. Permanently," said Doc.

Mabel and Fern exchanged glances. Fern shrugged. "Okay by me."

An elephantine snore almost powerful enough to rip the cloth bonnet from the wagon escaped Heather's respiratory system as she rolled over on one side.

"She sounds like she's going to sleep all the way to the Gulf," observed Fern. "Maybe we ought to try waking her up."

Down on her knees beside the sleeper, Mabel grasped Heather's shoulders and shook her violently. "Heather . . ."

Heather ignored her completely, rolling back over onto her back and continuing to torment their eardrums.

"That deep a sleep isn't healthy," said Doc professing concern. "It puts a strain on the heart."

Mabel got to her feet. "So wake her up." She swept the interior of the wagon with one hand. "With all this junk, all these patent medicines, you must have something that'll do it, without hurting her."

"Without killing her," added Fern.

Doc shrugged. "Maybe aromatic spirits of ammonia."

"So what are you waiting for?" exclaimed Fern. "Get at it!"

It was clear to Doc that both Mabel and Fern were becoming more and more worried. It did appear that nothing short of a twenty-one-gun salute fired off inside the wagon would bring Heather back to life. But instead of rummaging among his boxes and crates for spirits of ammonia, Doc turned his back on all three and climbed up onto the seat.

"Wake her up, goddamn you!" yelled Mabel.

His answer came back over his shoulder as he took the reins in hand and started Judith down the road.

"When we get to Kirkland. Let's give her a chance to come around by herself. Besides, if we need a doctor, there'll be one there."

He looked back a second time a few minutes later and saw Mabel and Fern kneeling on either side of the prostrate, still snoring Heather. The two stared at her, then looked at one another worriedly, Fern nervously biting her lower lip and shaking Heather gently by the shoulder.

Kirkland was not one of the larger settlements of northwestern Texas. Like so many places similar in size, it was essentially a Saturday-night gathering spot for the wheat and cotton farmers whose spreads surrounded it. There was a saloon, a general store, a half-finished church, a few nondescript shops, a sheriff's office, and a stable, but no telegraph office and nothing resembling a bank, and the only hotel appeared to be two floors of windows stacked above the saloon. It was, concluded Doc, a frontier-spawned community that was yet to begin growing, a widened space in the road on the way to Wichita Falls boasting fewer than fifty permanent residents.

Barely big enough to support a three-girl brothel.

Reining Judith to a stop in front of the general store, he climbed back into the wagon. Fern and Mabel were still down on their knees going through the motions of ministering to Heather, slapping her cheeks and wrists lightly, talking to her in persuasive tones.

"There's no change," said Fern worriedly. "She's sleeping herself to death, poor dear."

Mabel glared at Doc. "It's all your fault!"

"*My* fault?"

"You more than likely got your labels all mixed up and now she's full of chloroform! Murderer!"

"It's my fault she broke into my goods, sure. . . ."

"If you hadn't told her about the goddamn stuff in the first place . . ." began Mabel.

"Do something!" shrilled Fern.

"Okay, okay. Relax." He began poking through one box after another and eventually came up with a small bottle, slipping it unseen by either Mabel or Fern into his jacket pocket. Then he found a second, larger bottle.

"There's cotton in that gray box in the corner by the tailgate," he said pointing. "Give me a small piece."

Fern speedily did so, thrusting it into his hand. Uncorking the bottle, he placed the cotton over the top and shook the bottle once. Then he waved the wad under Heather's nostrils.

"What is that stuff?" queried Mabel.

"I already told you, aromatic spirits of ammonia. It'll bring her around."

Within seconds Heather stopped snoring. She lay still.

"She's stopped breathing!" exclaimed Mabel.

Fern screamed, her hands flying to her face. "She's dead!"

Doc gulped and, bending low over Heather's breasts, listened to her heart. "Jesus Christ . . ."

"What's the matter?"

"What!"

"Her heart, I think it's stopped." Straightening, he ordered the two of them up and out with wave. "Get a doctor! Fast as you can! Hurry!"

"But you're a doctor . . ." began Fern.

"I'm a damned druggist! Do as I tell you, go find a doctor! Quick! There's still time to save her!"

Instantly Mabel and Fern fell apart, jumping to their feet, jumping into each other, screaming, all but throwing themselves over the tailgate into the street and running off in opposite directions yelling hysterically for a doctor.

Moving to the rear of the wagon, Doc tossed their bulging carpetbags over the side, then scrambled back to Heather.

"Two down, one to go."

A small clutch of curious onlookers had begun assembling near the tailgate, peering inside. Dropping the rear flap and securing it to ensure privacy, Doc hauled his toolbox out from under the driver's seat, poked through it, and found what he needed, a grease pencil. He began dotting his forehead, cheeks, and chin with the pencil, speckling himself liberally. Then, producing the second bottle from his pocket, he uncorked it and began waving it back and forth under Heather's nose. She started, her head jerking, her face grimacing. In seconds she was wide awake, sitting up supported by his arm.

"Whaa . . . ? Where . . . ?"

"Easy, Heather, you're all right. You were asleep, I just brought you around. You're okay . . ."

She glanced about her. "Where's Mabel and Fern . . ." Pausing, she gaped. "What's the matter witn your face?"

"It's nothing."

"It's all red spots. What is it?"

"Nothing, relax. I'll be okay, I've had it before."

"What is it!"

"Nothing, I tell you . . ."

"Smallpox!" Heather blanched and all but swooned.

The canvas previously dropped and tied to the tailgate effectively cut off the Kirklander's view of the proceedings inside the wagon. But they could still hear. At the sound of the word, a woman screamed and instantly the crowd stampeded off.

"Smallpox," repeated Heather. "My God . . ."

"Take it easy, no need to get upset. Mabel and Fern went to get a doctor. I'll be okay. I've had it before." He grimaced. "I'm feeling a little sick to my stomach . . ."

He brought his other hand around and started to help her to her feet. But all this effort accomplished was to alert her to the fact that he already had one arm around her.

"Don't touch me!" She shrank back, pushing herself toward the tailgate. "Smallpox, it's . . . it's . . ."

"Contagious, but it's not so bad. The red spots don't last but a day or so. It's when they start erupting . . . the pock marks . . ." He moved toward her, his hands extended in appeal. "Help me over against the gate, will you? I'm beginning to feel weak all over. Untie that canvas drop, I need fresh air . . ."

"Don't come near me!"

In two seconds she had loosened one drop tie and was up and over the side—and running down the street like a well-scalded hound.

Tossing her bag over the tailgate, he rolled the canvas drop back up, secured it, moved forward, climbed back up onto the seat, and drove off.

Easing his handkerchief out of his breast pocket, he wet one corner of it with the tip of his tongue and proceeded to wipe the red spots from his face.

Then he extracted an Old Virginia from his pocket, lit it, and began drawing on it contentedly.

9

The Wells Fargo office in Wichita Falls resembled the one in Amarillo, even to the location of the safe, its door hanging by a single hinge. Most of the office furniture was likewise identical, desks overly abused, fancy carved-back wooden office chairs, and eighteen-inch oak stools for the two clerks. There was, however, no narrow hall-way leading to the supply room, rather a door opening directly into it. A more practical, if less private arrangement.

Mr. Hubert W. Pritchard, assistant to Mr. Hubbell, the murdered manager, was a thickset sort who displayed an interesting variety of shades of red—orange-red hair, florid cheeks, baby-lace-pink nose, and lips the color of the red ink scratched across the open cloth-bound ledger atop his desk. Mr. Pritchard struck Doc as an unusually nervous type, with no control whatsoever over his fluttering hands and flexing fingers. He fussed and fidgeted and generally disported himself in conversation with his investigating visitor like the primest prime suspect available.

The fact that Mr. Pritchard and the deceased got along like two cats in a burlap sack squabbling over one mouse—information volunteered by the local marshal—was sufficient cause for Mr. Pritchard's nervousness. And it took considerable time and all of Doc's not inconsiderable powers of persuasion to calm the man down to a point where his responses to questions became reasonably intelligible. The fact that the other employees had been sent home for the day, giving Doc and Pritchard privacy, helped the situation.

No, Pritchard had not been at the office the night of the crime. It had been Pritchard's custom, with Hubbell's permission, to take every Tuesday off to stay home and attend to his wife who, he assured Doc, was bedridden, suffering from pleurisy.

"Doc Sligh can tell you how serious her condition is."

"I'm sure he can. I believe you."

"Tuesday is Lucy, the hired girl's day off. We don't have any children."

Further questioning established that Pritchard had left the office at six o'clock the previous evening. The murder-robbery had taken place sometime before ten, the body discovered the next morning by Lucius Alsop, the office boy, whose job it was to open the office every morning.

"Lucius spotted Mr. Hubbell's body on the floor, the safe open. He locked the door immediately and came running over to my house. We went straight to the marshal. The three of us then went back to the office. Marshal Burrows sent Lucious home. He's only thirteen, we didn't think he ought to . . . you understand."

Pritchard then produced a note identical to the one found by Todd Massingale in the Amarillo Wells Fargo office. Same wording, same handwriting, even the same type of paper.

Doc read the note and pocketed it.

"One-hundred-and-eight thousand dollars was stolen," he said. "Right?"

"To the penny. I can show you the ledger right here. Mr. Weatherbee . . ."

"Sir?"

"I can prove I was home with Mrs. Pritchard at the time this dreadful business took place."

"I'm sure you can, Mr. Pritchard. I'm not worried about that."

"Do you have any idea who might have done such a terrible thing?"

Doc gestured helplessness. "I've only been in town an hour." He felt sorry for Pritchard, as he would have for any man living such a stressful life, and burdened in addition with an invalid wife. Doc's sense of fair play asserted itself, and in spite of his conviction that the home office would never approve, he filled Pritchard in on the specifics of the Amarillo case.

Pritchard heard him out and brightened considerably. "That means some outsider did it."

"We can't be absolutely certain, not a hundred percent, but it looks that way."

"I have to be honest with you, Mr. Weatherbee."

"Doc."

"Wilbur Hubbell and I weren't what you'd call the best of friends."

"Lots of people working together don't get along, Mr. Pritchard. But they rarely resort to murder. Particularly in such a gruesome way."

"We disliked each other intensely. He was always . . ." His voice trailed off. "I was on the verge of quitting half a dozen times. Our personalities clashed." He sighed. "Did they ever. But I never would have killed him. I'd never hurt a fly. I don't even have the stomach for rabbit hunting."

He had gotten his emotions under control now, his nervousness giving way to curiosity. "That's the thing that confuses me. Why do you suppose whoever did it chopped his head off?"

"I wish I knew. We're working on that angle." He smiled grimly. "And every other we can lay our hands on." Doc rose from his chair. "I have a camera and tripod outside in my wagon."

"What kind?" Pritchard's eyes came alive with interest. "I'm a bulb squeezer of sorts myself. Strictly amateur, of course."

"Mine's a Premo Senior."

"The big boy. Six-five-two-six . . ."

"That's it."

"I've got the Pony."

"Ever take pictures of your friends?"

"Mostly just family get-togethers."

"Ever take any of Wilbur Hubbell?"

"No thanks, I wouldn't waste the . . ." He paused and cleared his throat. "If you're looking for pictures of Wilbur, his wife Pauline's got a few scattered about the house."

"I was planning to stop in and see her."

"First house on the right heading south out of town. White clapboard. You can't mistake it; it looks three-quarters buried in rose bushes."

Doc glanced about, "I'll need shots of the office here, the furniture arrangement, the safe, what's left of it, I'll need all I can get of Hubbell, too."

Pritchard frowned and scratched the side of his head. "That may present a problem. He's been buried more than a week. Doc Sligh sort of insisted. He and the local undertaker got Pauline's permission. You'd have to open the grave."

"We will. We wouldn't want to leave any stone unturned. There's one favor you can do for me, if you wouldn't mind."

"Name it."

"Get ahold of your employees. Get them in here around, oh, let's make it four o'clock this afternoon. That'll give me time to get together with Mrs. Hubbell. I'll want to take everybody's picture, yours included. Then question them. As a group and singly."

"Yes sir, Mr. Weatherbee."

"Doc."

10

Doc took forty-three pictures of the office interior, including three of Hubert Pritchard, then stowed his camera, tripod, and negatives for developing that evening in the wagon and headed Judith south out of town for the Hubbell residence.

Pauline Hubbell, attired in widow's black, a bolero-style suit of serge cheviot, answered his knock at the door. Greeting him coolly, she examined his Pinkerton operative identification card with a quick glance, warmed up immediately, and showed him into the parlor, the taffeta lining of her skirt rustling like quail escaping a thicket.

Pauline Hubbell was, Doc adjudged, in her early sixties, a big-bosomed, big-boned, broad-shouldered Amazon with a smile that lit up her face only by dint of conscientious effort.

"Sit down" came out of her tight-lipped mouth as more command than invitation.

Doc glanced about the parlor. It was attractively, if excessively furnished, an elegant birch-finished suite in handsome imitation mahogany comfortably upholstered, edges fringed with silk gimp cord; a curly birch rocker distinguished by upholstered silk brocatel into which he had been ordered to sit, and various other pieces that fell noticably short of complementing the motif established by the suit.

At his elbow stood a jardiniére supporting an enormous brass pot overflowing with philodendron. The wall opposite featured a painting of an elk coming down to drink from a partially frozen stream, the frame finished in ivory enamel, with tinted edges of gold-tipped ornament that captured a shaft of the midafternoon sun, bouncing it against his appraising eye and all but blinding him.

Three imitation Dresden banquet lamps stood about on tables of varying sizes and construction. The porcelain parts of all three were decorated in floral designs. Terra-cotta tapestry curtains with knotted fringe tops framed all four windows, and underlaying the entire assembly was an Axminster rug with a scroll design large enough to wrap half a dozen Cleopatras for delivery to Caesar.

Mrs. Hubbell excused herself to "put tea on," and he sat alone fiddling with his derby, absorbing and consciously striving to be impressed by the mail-order splendor all about him. When the tea was ready, the lady reappeared bearing a hammered-brass tray cluttered with Haviland china.

"It's orange pekoe," she said in a demure tone, pro-nouncing the brand to rhyme with the word *echo*. "Im-ported from Kansas City. My favorite. Lemon or sugar?"

"Sugar, thank you."

"One lump or two?"

"Two, thank you."

They sipped in silence, her steely eyes glued to his face in expectation of approval.

"It's delicious," said Doc. It was not. It was dreadful, tepid, tasteless, and one of two small chips on the rim of his cup had already dug itself into his lip, threatening to slice the flesh wide open.

"You're here about Wilbur, aren't you," said Mrs. Hubbell, with no suggestion of grief on her face, in her eyes, in her voice. She set her half-consumed tea back on the tray. Taking a deep breath, she abruptly yielded to the urge to display great pain at her loss—an exhibition too tardy to make any impression on her visitor. Doc's eyes wandered to the framed photograph of a homely, bald-headed man in his sixties, his neck throttled in a Clarence collar so tightly fitted it appeared to be the sole cause of his bulging eyes. The picture perched atop a handsomely carved solid oak parlor organ concealing the wall under the painting of the elk. Setting cup and saucer on the jardi-niere, Doc got up and went to the portrait to examine it.

"A fine-looking gentleman, your husband."

She tittered. "He was homely as a mud fence. I've seen better-looking mules. Don't misunderstand. Far be it from me to speak ill of the dead, but you should have seen him alive. The photographer wiped out the bulbous growth at the corner of his nose and smoothed down his cheeks." She clucked disappointedly. "Take my word for it, my Wilbur was no Adonis."

The afternoon was rapidly extending itself in the direction of four o'clock. Pritchard's people would be gathering at the office to have their pictures taken and to be interrogated. Getting to the real reason for his visit seemed to be in order.

"With your permission, Mrs. Hubbell . . ."

"Pauline, please."

"If it wouldn't be inconvenient, could you let me borrow this or any other picture of your late husband?"

"There must be half a dozen strewn about the place. You can have them all if you like."

"Just one will do. I can have a copy made and return it to you."

She took the picture down, thrusting it into his hands. "Best take this one. He looks six times better than in any of the others."

"Thank you kindly, ma'am."

"Pauline."

"Pauline, yes. One other thing."

"Yes?"

She had finished her tea and was refilling both cups.

"I'll need your permission to open your husband's grave."

Her eyes widened as if pushed from behind, all but bursting free of their sockets, and her hand holding the teapot began trembling so that she nearly spilled the tea all over her Axminster.

"Mr. Weatherbee! Did I hear you correctly?"

"I beg your pardon, Pauline . . ."

"*Mrs*. Hubbell, if you don't mind!"

"I had no intention of shocking or upsetting you, but in order to solve this case, it's advisable we disinter your late husband's remains; more than advisable, actually absolutely necessary. We've got to photograph it . . . him, them . . ."

She dropped heavily into the rocker, jouncing her tea on its saucer and spilling a small quantity.

"No! Out of the question. We're staunch Baptists, Mr. Weatherbee. Once a loved one is dead and buried and his soul is released to heaven above, the very suggestion of . . . of opening up his sacred ground to snap photographs, of all things, is inconceivable! No, no, no!"

She got up and, turning her back on him walked slowly to the window. Any second now she would haul herself up to full height, glare frigidly, and order him out the door. He sneaked a peek at his watch. Allowing three minutes to get back to the Wells Fargo office, he had roughly twenty-two minutes to change her mind and get out of the place with her permission in writing.

He went to work. He began by inundating her with apologies, following up with a string of outrageously complimentary allusions to her person, her strength of character, her integrity, her wifely loyalty, her taste in furniture, her love of yellow roses—in particular those assaulting the front of the house in numbers roughly comparable to the hordes of Genghis Khan—her tea, and her charms. She rewarmed to him with astonishing rapidity, all but circling his waist with her arm and hugging him to her.

Sensing success within his grasp, he played his ace. Gesturing at the organ, he asked if she played.

"I dabble, I dabble. I adore music, don't you?"

"As Lord Byron so aptly put it: There's music in the sighing of the reed; there's music in the gushing of the rill; there's music in all things, if men had ears, their earth is but an echo of the spheres."

"How beautiful. How sensitive. Do you play?"

"I haven't the talent, worse luck. My only gift is in enjoying the performing of others. Would you play something for me, Pauline? Would it be too much trouble . . . ?"

Beaming, she swept to the organ, spreading her derrière practically the full width of the bench and launched at once into Blumenthal's "Flower Song."

She played wretchedly. Compared with her musical gifts, her tea was ambrosia. She had, alas, no ear for music. The organ was dreadfully out of tune, so far off key it would take, Doc mused, six tuners six weeks to bring it around to proper playing condition. Nevertheless, she hurled herself into the piece, her fat fingers flailing away at the keys, jerking and jamming the celluloid stop knobs and pounding the nickel-plated pedal frames with abandon.

Having finished at last, she spun about on the bench

and threw out her arms. Doc clapped and cheered loudly. "Encore, encore!"

"Let's try something modern," she said, clearing her throat.

He cringed. Christ, he thought, she's not going to sing. She isn't!

She sang "Her Golden Hair Was Hanging Down Her Back," three choruses, actually the one and only chorus repeated. This was followed by "My Love Wears a Rose Over Each of Her Ears," and "There Is a Garden in My Heart":

". . . and you hold the hoe of affection . . ."

The recital embraced the longest thirty minutes Doc had ever lived through. Apologizing for having to run off, he declared with a face as straight as he could manage that he had enjoyed her tea, her playing, and her singing immensely and wished with all his heart that he might stay and listen "till the cows come home,"—but duty called.

"Again, I do apologize for asking your permission to disinter your late husband. Technically speaking, he wouldn't be disinterred, nothing like it."

"If all you want to do is take pictures, wouldn't you just have to dig down, open the lid, and shoot?"

"Exactly. How evey perceptive of you, dear lady. Not a hand would be laid on him, nothing moved, nothing disturbed." He went into his standard General Principle explanation of the procedure, its need and its value, ending with "Thank you all the same. I understand and respect your feelings perfectly. Far be it from me to add to the burden of your grief . . ."

"Do it."

"I beg your pardon?"

"Open it up. Take all the pictures you like. If you think it'll help find his murderer."

"It will, I can almost guarantee it will." Doc produced a form letter from his inside jacket pocket. "Ahem, I will need your signature on the bottom line."

She read the few lines of the form and patted his cheek. "I'll fetch pen and ink."

"Thank you kindly." said Doc. "I'll fill in the details later."

He watched her sail off into the bedroom to get the pen

and inkwell. He shook his head dejectedly. Between hitchhiking whores and winsome widows with tin ears whose cooperation in their own best interests was, in their opinion, as demanding as giving birth, working for Allan Pinkerton could certainly get a conscientious man like Doc Weatherbee down—particularly in light of the confusion that was rapidly beginning to flourish. A murder in Amarillo, a prime suspect purportedly holed up somewhere in No Man's Land, a second all but identical killing in Wichita Falls . . .

If any of it had made any sense to start with, it seemed to be making a lot less at the moment.

He rode away from Pauline Hubbell's house arranging things to be done in order of priority. Back to the office to question the employees. To the local undertaker to talk about Wilbur Hubbell, show the undertaker the permission form signed by Pauline, pick up a supply of film, visit the cemetery, open the grave, and take a half-dozen beauty shots of the corpse. Then, perhaps, between supper and bedtime while he was busy developing his photos, summon Hubert Pritchard for one final chat and get him to divulge the real reason why he was carrying on in such an outrageously guilty manner.

For a man with an alibi comfortably clad with iron, Mr. Hubert Pritchard, self-confessed lifelong enemy of the deceased, was behaving very very strangely.

11

Raider, meanwhile, continued making his way toward Beaver, digging snow pockets for himself and his horse and warming them with buffalo-chip fires, fuel fetched along from Titus Z. Campbell's collapsed barn. As the days passed, the sun brightened, melting the residue of the blizzard and bringing Raider within sight of the Jones and Plummer trail slicing north to south from Kansas through No Man's Land to Texas. And squatting on the trail where it came upon the North Canadian River was Beaver.

The town was roughly the size of Boise City, but was decidedly less civilized, for this was part of Comanche country, which ranged west and south along both sides of the Palo Duro Creek. Raider's first stop in town was at the Jim Lane Store, a modest little house with a shingle roof, a brick chimney, and an addition in the rear nestling comfortably in a blanket of soot-stained snow a foot deep in places, six and more where the wind had piled it against the addition.

At Jim Lane's he warmed his innards with Valley Tan and hot beef stew, had his horse fed and watered, increased his dwindling supply of traveling grub, and scouted out the town. In addition to Jim Lane's place there was a Presbyterian church, a new stable going up, a telegraph office, and a courthouse with the sheriff's office occupying the ground floor, where among the faces posted on the bulletin board out front was that of Lock Flanagan— "Wanted for Robbery and Murder." Wells Fargo's interest in his arrest and conviction was underscored by an offer of $1,000 reward—which, reflected Raider, amounted to only one eighty-fifth of the missing Amarillo money.

The sheriff filling a sheepskin coat and shiny new boots was a young man, blubbery heavy for his limited years, tired-eyed, his words muffled by a strange mumble, as if his tongue were too big for his mouth.

"Yeah, yeah, we know Flanagan's supposed to be around here," he said in response to Raider's mention of the name. "We knew it before Wells Fargo found out." He sat atilt in a barrel-back chair angled against the wall beside the courthouse door. He stared disapprovingly at Raider astride the bay, as if his riding into Beaver uninvited was about as welcome as a plague of black flies in August. "But we ain't got the manpower to mount no posse. I got me one full-time deputy and a fella comes in every afternoon to sweep and swamp out the place and can strap a gun on if he got to, but rather shit than shoot. This ain't Oklahoma City, you know."

"I'm not asking for your help, Sheriff," said Raider evenly, "leastwise not guns and riding out." Dismounting, he patted his horse affectionately and leaned across the saddle on his forearms staring back at the man in the awkwardly tilted chair. "I'm only interested in any information you might have."

The sheriff jerked his thumb at the wanted poster. "If you can read, that's it. I can give you some pretty good advice, though."

"Yeah?"

"My advice is to get back up on your horse and go on back to where you come from."

"Is that an order, General?"

"I said it was advice. You're wastin' your time lookin' for Flanagan 'round these parts."

"That's mighty peculiar advice, seeing as this is where he's supposed to be at. It could even be why you hung his dodger up there. . . ."

"He could be upstairs sleepin' on Judge Fraily's siesta couch; that don't mean you're gonna be the lucky boy who's gonna collect his ass."

"That thousand-buck reward must look pretty good to you."

The sheriff scowled and unloaded one nostril between his boots. "You think I'm worried some outside slob like you is gonna collect it? Mister, you got to be dumber than a one-eyed turkey cock. It could be a thousand, it could be a hundred thousand, that there is one ree-ward ain't nobody gonna collect, not you or me or nobody."

"You sound awful sure."

"You bet your balls I'm sure. If you really got to

know, my number-one deputy, Leland P. Boggs, happens to have got the word firsthand from a Kiowa Apache friend that Flanagan is runnin' with a bunch o' Comanches, Blue Wolf's crowd. The fact of the matter is, Flanagan has took hisself a fuckin' squaw for his bride and is now a honorary member of Blue Wolf's pack, what you might say outta touch with Pale-eyes civilization permanent-like." He paused, smirked, cocked his fat head to one side and squinted at Raider from under the brim of his Stetson. "Is any o' this gettin' through to you?"

"Most of it."

"Good boy."

"What I mean is, if you didn't talk like you had two goddamn tongues in your mouth, it'd come out and get through a damn sight better, Mr. Fat Bat Masterson!"

"Why you wiseass son of a bitch . . ."

His face reddening, the sheriff started up out of his chair. He failed to make it. Sitting tilted at such an extreme angle, the effort to rise pulled the left front leg out from under him, collapsing man and chair in a heap.

"Ow! Ouch! Goddammit!"

Raider mounted and rode off at an easy lope, looking back once only, pleased and amused at the sight of the sheriff gripping his left ankle, his face twisted with pain and cursing at the top of his voice.

12

Raider reported his arrival in Beaver and word that Lock Flanagan was running with the Comanches by way of telegram carefully encoded and clicked through to Amarillo. A response from Doc at Wichita Falls reaching Amarillo earlier was relayed to Beaver within the hour. The blank wall the two of them had come up against in Amarillo was, according to Doc, duplicated in Wichita Falls. Minor differences in the two cases, the fact that Wilbur Hubbell had left a widow, had had an assistant who hated him, and had only been managing the Wichita Falls Wells Fargo office for seventeen months were of no real importance to the investigation. At least, as Doc pointed out in his message, at this point.

Sitting in his long johns in a squalid little room in the White House Hotel in Beaver, cleaning his .44 and submerging both feet in a basin filled with hot water laced with Epsom salts, Raider wiggled his corn-afflicted and well-callused toes and considered the present status of the case.

Evidence at hand was meager; the area surrounding Beaver, reaching up into Kansas and down into Texas, was half the size of Arkansas, the weather temporarily fair but once again become freezing cold. If the sheriff's deputy's story was straight, Flanagan was probably working with Comanche braves, hitting settlements and running —and sneaking in an occasional Wells Fargo office to relieve the monotony as well as to savor his revenge. Indians had been known to slip into towns by night and raise hell, loot and burn, and get out before the residents got the sleep out of their eyes and their boots hauled on.

But getting the Comanches, of all tribes, to assist him in revenging his younger brother's death, was an accomplishment worthy of any man's admiration. Even a Pinkerton's.

The Cheyennes were tall, as were the Crows, Blackfeet, and Kiowas; the Pimas were runty, the Comanches only slightly taller. Lock Flanagan, standing halfway to seven feet, would stick out in a raiding party like a totem pole in the midst of a bundle of hog sty posts.

Raider knew the Comanches well. In his mind's eye he could see their faces as bright as copper, their long black hair ornamented with glass beads and silver gewgaws.

They were not stupid-looking like the Quapawa and the Santee Sioux. To Raider, the latter all looked alike, moon-faced moose with mouths perpetually hanging open.

The Comanches had thin lips, aquiline noses, eyes dark brown and black, and little chin hair. The hair on their heads never seemed to get gray, no matter how old, wrinkled, and creaky they became. A rumor had circulated for years that the Comanches' eyes were weaker than those of other Indians. If this was true, it appeared to have little effect on their marksmanship. The Spanish arriving in the Americas had taken their hunting grounds and their women, but had given them the horse. Rather the Comanches had taken it. In time their braves had become the most skillful riders in North America. Using a bow of Osage orangewood, they could drive a mulberry shaft tipped with a flinthead into the lean area just behind a buffalo's short rib with astonishing accuracy. At ten yards a Comanche brave could put ten arrows out of ten through an equivalent number of full-grown bulls, 1,500 pounds on the hoof, dropping them dead in their tracks. Since the war the Comanche had become even more adept with a rifle, anything from a rusty Henry to a Sharps, Remington, Winchester, any stock and barrel with trigger between, shooting one-handed, galloping forty miles an hour, loading and reloading on the run with the dexterity of a jeweler popping a precious stone into its setting.

Raider readily admitted to himself that he could not ride in pursuit of or away from a party of Comanches if his life depended on it. A test of this appeared to be a reasonable future possibility that rankled him no little.

The Sioux had an ingrained dread of being ambushed, preferring to camp near water but away from timber; the Arapahos and the Cheyennes preferred the open prairie but near timber; the Shawnees, Omahas, and Osages looked for thickets, the denser the better.

The Comanches liked a running stream near open woodland, along undulating creek valleys toward the headwaters of larger streams, where canyons were located, arroyos and other rocky arrangements offering natural protection. They took excellent care of their mounts and therefore consistently sought abundant grass. For themselves, they looked for buffalo and antelope.

Unlike some tribes, particularly the Hidatsas and Mandans in North Dakota and the Chippewas in Minnesota, the Comanches did not winter-quarter, in the sense of settling down in their lodges like bears in their caves to wait for spring. They hunted, as did all the tribes at all times, with the exception of the soil tillers. But the Comanches also made war, all year round—with any tribe similarly inclined or white settlers, inclined or not. Making life miserable for their neighbors was more than an enjoyable pastime, more even than an honorable endeavor for the Comanches; it was, in spite of the claims of their admirers and apologists, their religion.

Raider wiggled his toes and stretched his feet, laying aside the .44, digging out his Sears Roebuck Ivory Tang straight razor and detaching a large and lately somewhat troublesome corn from his right big toe.

However reluctantly, he had to give Flanagan high marks for courage and common sense. Joining Blue Wolf's people, cementing the relationship by becoming a squaw man in order to work his grisly mischief against Wells Fargo, was inspired thinking.

To catch the bastard, separate him from his redskin friends and his bride, and bring him in looked to be about as easy as fucking a turkey buzzard on the wing: "With both hands tied behind my goddamn back!"

For the next two weeks Raider stayed clear of Beaver's sheriff and his deputy and a half, and circuit-rode the surrounding area, asking questions of sodbusters, wheat farmers, sheepmen and cattlemen, and more than one lone Kiowa brave, to whom he showed Lock Flanagan's sketched likeness, unfolding and refolding the paper until it came apart in quarters and from then on had to be exhibited laid on a rock or whatever was handy, pieced together to form the face.

On Monday of the final week of January, the coin of

luck flipped over. In a sod saloon in a small settlement called Mayo, just up the North Canadian River from Fort Supply, Raider was sitting alone at a crudely constructed wooden table so small he could almost cover the top of it with his hat, drenching his disappointment with rye whiskey that tasted almost as bad as it smelled, when a stranger came striding up to him, elevated the greasy brim of his hat, and, seizing the stool opposite, sat down.

Few patrons were in attendance at such an early hour of the morning. The owner, tending bar—two twelve-foot plants supported by a cracker barrel at either end—sang to himself and assiduously wiped the dust from one unlabeled bottle after another, preparatory to capping them with a funnel and filling them with rotgut.

"How much money you offerin' for information about Lock Flanagan?" inquired the stranger, lowering his voice and glancing first left, then right out of the corners of his bloodshot eyes. The man reeked of horse manure, decided Raider, stifling a wince. On second thought, mule manure. Having shared the driver's seat of Doc's wagon behind Judith for many miles, Raider felt qualified to distinguish between the two odors, however unimportant this intelligence may have been.

"Who's Lock Flanagan?" asked Raider. "Who might you be?"

"Names don't mean nothin'," said the smelly one. "Who are you?"

"Jesus Christ Almighty. In disguise."

"I ain't here to make jokes with you, friend. The word is you're lookin' for Flanagan and I happen to know where he is. I mean right now today, not tomorry or next week, on account he moves around. You give me fifty bucks cash money and I'll tell you where he's at." With this he held out one grimy hand, wiggling the three fingers still attached to it in a hand-it-over gesture.

"Would I be hurting your feelings any if I asked you to get up from this table and take your stink someplace else?" asked Raider in the politest tone he could muster.

"Sticks and stones can hurt my bones, but names don't hurt nothin'. Fifty dollars cash money."

Raider emptied his glass, set it down, and began turning it slowly, aimlessly in place. "You've seen him?" he asked quietly.

"Bet your boots."

"How did you know it was him?"

"I reckynized him. From the describin' . . ."

Raider took out the four quarters of the artist's sketch and pieced them together on the table. "Is this him?"

"In the flesh."

"You're sure."

"Sure as I'm sittin' here."

"Short party, say five-foot-six or seven?"

"Taller'n that. I'd say more five-eight or nine."

"Big belly . . . ?"

"Big. Big."

"How big?"

"Bigger'n a blue-ribbon sow."

Raider nodded and tried to look impressed. "How was he walking?"

A blank expression crept into the bloodshot eyes. "Walkin'?"

"With a limp, right?"

"Yeah, with a limp. I forgot about that limp."

"Left leg or right?"

"Let me see, I reckon it was his left. But it coulda been his right. I was standin' behind him and it was hard to tell. He wasn't doin' much walkin', just sorta' standin'."

"It sure sounds like Lock Flanagan."

"It is!" Down came the flat of the man's hand against the sketch. "That's him. . . . Fifty bucks, that's all I'm askin'." Turning his hand over, he resumed asking with it.

"First you got to tell me where he's at."

"Oh no you don't. First the fifty, then I tell."

"You're a hard man to do business with."

"A fella's got to take his advantages when they comes."

"I'll tell you what." Raider got up. "You stick here, I'll go back and talk it over with my four partners. If they agree, we'll pay you the fifty. Only you're gonna have to lead us to him before you can collect."

"Forget that!"

"Why not? Fair's fair."

"I ain't about to buy no back fulla Comanche arrers, thank you kindly. I'll tell you where he's at, I'll point out the spot from, say, a mile away. Safe distance. You pay me, then you five ride in and grab his ass."

"That's the way you want it, huh?"

"That's the way it's got to be. A man earns hisself fifty dollars, he got to stay alive to spend it, don't he?"

"Seems so." Raider picked up the pieces of the sketch and pocketed them. "Wait here, I'll be back in six hours."

"Six hours!"

"Sure, I got to round up my four partners. That should take till the middle of the afternoon, at least. Then we got to talk it over. I got to talk 'em into the deal. Mind you, that's no problem, but it'll take time. Everything takes time. Let's be on the safe side and make it seven hours. You wait here."

"For seven hours? Jesus, mister . . ."

"It may not be that long. It could turn out only an hour."

The man pulled his hat off and began fussing with it. And frowning.

"Make it fast as you can, will you?"

"We will, we will. Just be patient."

"Don't forget to bring the cash."

"I won't. Just you be here when we get here."

"I will, cross my heart."

"We can't be waiting around; this is a big-sized manhunt we got going for us."

Raider paid for his bottle, took it along, and rode out of Mayo. Even before the smelly stranger had joined him at the table, Raider's instincts were beginning to persuade him that he was chasing around the wrong woods. Not a single person he had talked to had recalled any six-foot-seven white man riding alone, let alone with Comanches. Not in Harper County and not east of Beaver situated in the center of the county of the same name.

Blue Wolf was known, but he hadn't been seen in the area recently either.

Maybe, reasoned Raider he ought to haul stakes and cross the border, try down along the Palo Duro Creek in Texas. He could give it at least as far south as Spearman. Even back in the direction of Boise City. Or north, up into Liberal or Elkhart. The Comanches were scattered all over the place. But Blue Wolf and his Irish acquisition could only be in one place at a time.

Change of scenery, change of luck.

Little did Raider realize as he rode off, the odor of the stranger gradually diminishing in his nostrils, that that very afternoon business would be, as the drummer would say, picking up.

13

Raider asked his way eastward back across No Man's Land, but not after Lock Flanagan. Instead he inquired as to the whereabouts of Blue Wolf and his people. A white buffalo hunter who looked around ninety, but was probably closer to fifty, heard him out on the trail outside of Turpin and directed him across the county line.

The man's wooden false teeth didn't fit too well and his explanation made more saliva than sense, but the gist of it was that the blizzard had caught Blue Wolf and his tribe short on food; most of the braves had been too busy battling settlers encroaching on their hunting grounds to chase down meat for the winter.

An hour later Raider ran across a Comanche hunting party. From the concealment of a snowdrift he watched the Indians pass three quarters of a mile away heading northwest—the direction suggested by his ancient acquaintance.

The Comanches, he knew, did not relish nice fat boiled puppy dogs like the Sioux and the Cheyennes, only because the dog is cousin to the coyote, which is taboo as nourishment. The coyote was the practical joker of Comanche and Shoshone mythology, a sort of subgod. On rare occasions the Comanches hunted the coyote for its fur, but they never ate its meat.

Their taste in meat ran to buffalo found on the open prairies, the ancestors of the hordes of yesteryear. Elk, their second choice, was abundant in the bush-bearing regions bordering rivers and streams. The Comanches also hunted the black bear, mostly for his grease, used in preparing hides. But they much preferred buffalo, elk, and antelope to bear meat. Only the white man's steer beef tasted worse to them than bear. Still, the bear's fur and his oil came in very handy; then too, removing an enemy rugged enough to claw two full-grown braves to death at the same time made good sense.

Raider counted close to thirty braves in the party. Considering the weather, their kill had been a good one, although there was nothing like drifted snow for slowing down a lumbering bull buffalo, and his loyal cow by his side. The meat they had taken was bagged in the hides and loaded on pack horses. And was being toted back to camp for further butchering.

Butchering at the kill site was a hasty and often dangerous affair. A brave, down on his knees slicing up a cow on her side or a bull heaved over onto his belly, all four legs spread, slashed their briskets at the neck and folded back the hide to the forequarters to facilitate their removal at the joint. Step by step the meat was quickly freed and stuffed in its hide bag, but while the whole procedure took only a few minutes, the brave wielding the knife was too busy to stay alert to danger. So every ten seconds or so he would flash a look at his horse's ears. The Comanches trained their animals to flip-flop their ears alternately if another buffalo or coyote started closing in. If a man tried to sneak up, the horse would pitch both ears forward.

This knowledge crossing his mind, Raider flattened himself upon the icy ground, permitting the hunting party to continue on its way without so much as one more glance from him.

He waited fifteen minutes in the freezing cold, his horse pulled down on its side wall-eyeing him questioningly, his hand over its muzzle to prevent its voicing protest. Then he mounted up and picked up the party's trail, staying a good four miles behind. On a clear day like this, any Indian, even the reputedly weak-eyed Comanche, could see miles and miles across the table-flat prairie. In every direction. Fortunately, what little wind was up was blowing straight at the party, carrying their scent and that of their meat back toward him.

The sun settled into the horizon, dissolving like the yolk of an egg, spreading left and right. Twilight seized and softened the landscape. Among the Comanches passing, Raider would have loved to have spied six feet seven inches of white man garbed in buffalo robes, singularly distinctive attire. Plainsmen and soldiers stationed at frontier forts insisted that one buffalo robe was warmer than four blankets. So Flanagan would be sure to be wearing one.

All in all, every member of the party looked a good deal warmer and more comfortable than the Pinkerton operative following them felt. The disappearance of the sun, the rising wind, the night cold taking possession of Raider's bones, body, and breath brought this unhappy reflection to mind and kept it there.

He estimated their traveling time, the pace slowed by the overburdened pack ponies, as upwards of three hours before dots of orange broke the blackness of the night and the quarter moon sickling the stars free of their unseen stalks revealed the conical shapes of tepees. They were supported by cedar poles, cut, peeled, patiently seasoned, pared down to proper diameter, and pointed at the butt to permit them to be sunk into the ground like tent stakes. From ten to seventeen buffalo hides were generally required to cover an average-sized tepee. As many as fourteen people shared the interior.

It was ironic, when Raider thought about it. The Comanches not only killed the buffalo, took him apart, and put his tastiest meat inside them, but then wound up living inside what was left of the poor fucking thing!

He counted twenty eight tepees, every one blowing smoke from its smokehole near the top, above the entrance. By the time he had ventured close enough to reckon the size of the camp, the hunters had already turned their meat over to the squaws for final butchering.

"Good for you, folks," he said to himself aloud, dismounting and lashing the bay to the limb of a tree, crouching and taking in the burst of activity prompted by the hunting party's arrival. Grass-green envy shared his hunger in the storeroom of his stomach as he sat down to a fireless supper of cold red beans and hard biscuit as dry and tasteless as sawdust and rendered no more palatable or even chewable by drenching with water from his canteen.

Squatting on his blanket roll munching away disconsolately, he found himself wishing to high heaven and humble hell that instead of Flanagan's picture he had one of Blue Wolf. He didn't need a picture to pick out a white man a foot taller than all the Indians around him. What he could really use were six close-up Doc Weatherbee special photographs of the chief.

He nevertheless had the feeling that this camp was *the* camp, that in one of those twenty-eight tepees Lock Flanagan and his bride were either sharing sex, enjoying buffalo steak, or engaging in friendly conversation with the overgrown hit-and-run killer's Comanche in-laws.

14

Raider's horse, hungry as usual, awoke him before dawn, pawing the frozen ground and nuzzling his face. Raider came to consciousness feeling like a block of ice clear down to his heels. Christ, what he wouldn't give for a half gallon of hot coffee, but even the thought of building a fire this close to two hundred Comanches was enough to jangle the nerves in his spine.

He fed the horse all the oats he had left, having come away from Beaver spurred by impulse and ignoring the necessity of resupplying himself for the trail. He guessed that he was less than fifty miles from Boise City. To ride there, stock up on supplies, and return would be taking a chance he was in no position to take. Blue Wolf, Flanagan, and the rest could be planning to tie down here for the rest of the winter, or until noon; there was no possible way to ascertain how long. To locate them only to ride away made no sense at all.

If indeed this was Blue Wolf's camp. The old-timer had led him to believe it was somewhere in the vicinity. But whether he had dreamed it or knew it for a fact was a moot point.

The sun rose, reluctantly, it seemed to Raider, as if undecided about expending any effort to chase the chill of yet another winter day. The sky wore a deathly gray color, but it was not a snow sky, nothing like the sullen overcast preceding the blizzard that had ushered Raider into No Man's Land.

The Comanches' camp came to life, the squaws emerging, stretching, yawning, their robes pulled tightly about them against the bitter cold. They started their buffalo-chip fires and fanned them to life, and squatted and stirred their cooking pots. The children and the men appeared eager for breakfast, stabbing pointed sticks into the pots and kettles, skewering meat, cooling it by waving it

back and forth or dragging it through a patch of snow,
then bolting it down.

The sight set Raider's stomach rumbling and his mouth
watering. But as he crouched watching, his heart jumped
at the sight of a giant white man in Stetson and boots with
a buffalo robe wrapped tightly about him with a gunbelt.
With him was a slim-looking bronzed beauty of a girl who
looked to be barely out of her teens. Side by side, the
top of her head failed by a good four inches to come up
to the height of his shoulder.

It was like matching a full-grown bull buffalo with an
antelope doe, reflected Raider. Even at this distance,
however, he could see that Flanagan had plucked himself
a rare flower. Her eyes were jet black and enormous,
her skin as lovely and flawless as any woman any color
Raider had ever seen; high cheekbones, little-girl breasts
under her robes, and a posture and walk as regal and
as straight-backed proud as Raider could imagine any
Boston socialite bride.

The artist who had sketched Flanagan had done justice to the man's hair and face. His measurements scribbled
on the back of the picture, however, woefully under-
estimated his size. He looked to be more like six-ten than
six-seven, close to 260 pounds, even 270. And all muscle,
his tightly cinched gunbelt allowing no room for a liquor
gut. Raider made a mental note. Whatever the future held
at all costs, he must avoid hand-to-hand combat with this
monster. By all appearances, Flanagan could break his
neck with one hand and his back with the other without
even bothering to take a deep breath.

Raider observed all morning long, and it became ap-
parent to him that Flanagan either was not allowed to or
did not choose to leave the camp alone. Blue Wolf and his
shaman walked off with him to talk about something
shortly before noon. A half-hour later Flanagan and his
wife went for a short ride, circling the camp at a distance.
There looked to be no chance for Raider to get close to
the big man unaccompanied by somebody or other.

The Comanches had staked and hobbled their horses
on the far side of the camp. To the left, a semicircle of
tepees marched toward the corral. Flanagan and his
squaw occupied the third tepee in the line; and as far as

Raider could make out, the two of them had it all to themselves.

Raider decided to wait until dark, hope for an overcast sky, give the tribe time to fall asleep, circle the camp, approach Flanagan's tepee, cut his way in, silence her with his gun to Flanagan's head, force the Irishman to bind and gag her, and ride away with his prisoner.

"It sounds so easy," he murmured to his horse. "Too easy to work."

The bay paid no attention. It was shivering with the cold and working its jaw hungrily, somehow seeming to sense that its next meal wasn't included in the schedule of events for the day. Or the night.

"How can you be hungry, you son of a bitch, you just ate!"

Raider wondered how far a hungry man could ride a hungrier horse in this lovely weather. It was fifty miles to Boise City, providing he, Raider, would be able to collect Flanagan and ride him out without two hundred Comanches on their tails. Could he pull it off?

Jesus Christ! Why hadn't he taken an extra half-hour to stock up? Doc would have. Would have taken all the time he needed to write down everything in a foot-long list and go out and get it. Judith ate like a four-legged queen, thanks to Doc's care, consideration, and old maid schoolmarm's penchant for detail.

But Raider wasn't Doc and the bay wasn't Judith, and he hoped that next time—if the two of them got through this time—he'd have enough horse sense to make proper preparations.

He tried feeding the bay some of his cold beans and biscuit, but it wanted neither, spitting out the biscuit so fast one would have thought it was poisoned.

One of the year's shortest days passed like one of its longest, but eventually darkness drove away the gray light, arriving moonless, without a single star, a solid black cloud blanketing the firmament. It got so dark so early that had it not been for the dying cooking fires spotted about the area, Raider, standing less than 150 yards distant, would have had trouble seeing any of the tepees, let alone picking out Flanagan's.

Securing the bay to a tree tunk and advising it in friendly tone to "keep quiet or you just may get a damn Comanche lance up your asshole," Raider started a wide circle away from the camp, determined to approach Flanagan's tepee from the east, belly down fifteen yards or so from it, wriggle his way across the remaining distance, listen for snoring, hope that he heard it, cut in and take his man.

His approach circle was so wide he fancied he was closing in on the Kansas border when he at last completed it and started straight toward the semicircle of tepees. Squinting through the blackness, he picked out the third in line, got close, down on his belly, shivering at the icy contact, and creeping up to the teepee, cut his way inside.

It was easy. It was quick. It caught the occupants completely by surprise.

It also surprised Raider.

It was the wrong tepee. . . .

"You'll be riding bareback."

"You're kidding'."

Raider cocked his gun. "Get your horse."

Flanagan was breathing hard, clenching and unclenching his fists. Raider could see the hate building in his face, the unmistakable look of liking to break him in half.

But he obeyed, kneeling beside a stallion nearly half again the size of Raider's bay, releasing its hobbles and swinging up onto its back. Raider cut the rein rope of the mare nearest it and mounted. Then he threw Flanagan's .45 as far away as he could.

They rode to where the bay was tied and Raider changed horses. He wished to hell he could free all the Comanches' mounts, cut all the hobbles, all the stake ropes. Scatter the whole herd. But there was no time.

He debated, too, switching the bay for the grulla mustang he'd cut from the group. But he didn't have the heart to leave his horse with a bunch of savages; it had served him too well too long.

"Where we goin'?" inquired Flanagan matter-of-factly.

"Boise City."

"How come? For chrissakes, you can at least tell me what it's all about."

"Put your hands behind your back."

Flanagan shrugged and crossed his wrists behind his rump. Raider tied his hands exactly as he had tied Haber Selkirk's on the night of the big blowup, permitting Flanagan to lead him by the length of his lariat.

They headed west. The wind came up, punishing and purpling their faces. Flanagan's horse appeared to be enjoying the dead-of-night canter. In comparison, Raider's bay was finding each succeeding mile more rugged than the one previous, half filling its lungs with short, desperate gasps, trembling as if at any moment it was goin to stop short, drop its forelegs under its chest, and pitch its rider head overhead.

"Slow down, Flanagan," called Raider. "We got all the time in the world."

"Not with two hundred redskins on your tail you ain't."

"Nobody back there's going to miss us till sunup."

"You sure you got the right man?"

"Loughlin Flanagan."

"You one .o' Hazlett's deputies?"

"Hazlett?"

"The sheriff over to Boise City."

"Oh yeah, his name slipped my mind."

"You ain't. Then what in blue hell are you, some roach-crotched bounty huntin' prick?"

"I'm with the Pinkerton Detective Agency."

"Pinkerton?" The word was uttered in a tone of complete mystification. Toeing his horse under both its shoulders, Flanagan slowed it to a trot. Raider slowed the bay in step. Flanagan turned his head and shook it. "Now I know you got the wrong man. Right name, wrong man. What's supposed to be the charge, Mr. Pink?"

"Murder and robbery."

"Who and what? And where?"

Raider explained.

Flanagan laughed at the sky. "Mister Pink, you are stark, ravin' nuts. You ain't just been chewin' peyote, you been swallyin' it!"

"Let's cut the bullshit short, shall we? All I'm supposed to do is take you in and get you behind bars. The rest is up to Hazlett and Wells Fargo and sixteen other parties."

"You'll be fuckin' lucky to get me to Boise City, let alone the rest of it. That horse o' yours sounds like it's ready to keel over an' die. We ain't even halfway there yet, you know that, don't you?"

"If this horse can't make it, then I'll ride yours and walk you in," said Raider quietly. "Keep moving."

16

The bay was giving its all, but had little left to give—
on an empty stomach, in this bitter cold, after so many
weeks of strenuous riding. Raider could well imagine how
close to total exhaustion it was getting; he himself was not
far behind.

So worried was he that he got down and began walking the horse as they neared the few feeble lights identify-
ing Boise City.

"Good boy. We'll get you a warm bed of hay and a
bellyful of feed. All the rest you can use, a week without
shifting a hoof, if you like. . . . Slow it down, Flanagan."

But with the lights of the town beginning to puncture
the darkness, Flanagan seemed to be getting ideas—in
view of the fact that he had managed to stretch the rope
binding his wrists and was within moments of slipping
loose.

He did it, freeing himself, heeling his horse fit to cave
in the animal's ribs and pounding away at a gallop. He
was thirty yards away, fast making it forty by the time
Raider got his mind onto what was happening, his .44 up
and shooting. Two hurried shots. Both caught the stallion
full in the left buttock. Its left hind leg caved in, dropping
Flanagan to the ground hard. Rolling over on all fours, he
shook out the cobwebs and glared at Raider.

"You fuckin' prick bastard!" He glanced at his horse
writhing in agony. "You stinkin' Pink son of a bitch! I'll
kill you for this! Don't just stand there, goddamn ya,
shoot him! Put him out of his misery."

Raider was already running forward, ignoring Flanagan, passing the stallion twisting its injured leg in agony,
whining loudly and struggling to rise. Its eyes were as
white and wide as china saucers.

Raider put a single shot into its forehead. It twitched. It
died.

"Best goddamn animal I ever did own," snarled Flanagan, getting to his feet and rubbing his hip and ribcage where he had landed on the hard ground.

"I wasn't aimin' for the horse," said Raider.

"You're a lousy fuckin' shot, Mr. Pink."

Raider pretended not to hear, thumbing the cylinder and cocking, reloading the two emptied chambers. He was heavy at heart at the sight of the dead horse lying at his feet. *What a waste,* he thought, *what a goddamn stupid waste . . .*

One man's preoccupation with anything is another's opportunity. Flanagan saw it and seized it; he came at Raider, butting him in the midsection, knocking him flat, coming up on his knees astride him, swinging two fists the size of Poland Chester hams. His left caught Raider on the side of the head, driving his brain clear to the right of its pan and halfway out his ear, or so it felt. Flanagan's right quickly sent it back the other way, just as fast, just as painfully. The blackness enveloping Raider's head came speedily, two shades darker than the night surrounding them. But though his brain quietly exploded, roiling the juices in which it was suspended, he somehow managed to cling to consciousness.

Satisfied that his two quick licks had effected all the damage needed, Flanagan pushed off, reaching for Raider's gun, which had fallen to one side when he had butted him to the ground. Freed of the big man's weight, Raider shook off the pain, rolled over, pulled himself up to his knees, and tackled Flanagan around the waist, at the same time pushing him forward into the ground. Flanagan's forehead hit.

The ground was as hard as his fists; the force of impact was like two tombstones toppling against each other. Raider lurched to his feet, took one look, breathed a sigh of relief, sent his hands up to the sides of his head to make sure nothing gray and wet was seeping out, pulled them down dry, and passed out.

He was lucky. He woke up before Flanagan did, nuzzled into consciousness by the bay. His head felt three times its ordinary size and a bell rang inside with the insistent regularity of the Methodist church steeple bell in Boise City he'd heard as he'd ridden away on Christmas Day.

Holstering his gun, he triple-tied Flanagan's wrists be-hind his back, slapped him awake, lifted him to his feet with the muzzle of the .44 buried in the softness of his chin, brought the weapon around to the nape of his neck, and walked him into town leading his loyal bay behind.

17

Getting Lock Flanagan behind the bars of one of Sheriff Barney Hazlett's cells combined feelings of relief, satisfaction, and something like pure joy in Raider's breast. These feelings were to be almost equaled by the sight of the bay stumbling shivering into the local stable and turned over to a large-hearted and sympathetic stableman who solemnly promised to care for the creature with the concern and attention he would lavish on a "new-dropped foal."

Best of all, though, was the stroke of heaven-sent luck that came Raider's way upon his return to the sheriff's office. A careful search of Flanagan's clothing, carried out while Hazlett and four of his deputies held him down, disclosed a money belt wrapped around the big man's chest.

In it was more than a hundred thousand dollars in bills.

Raider, Hazlett, and the four deputies stood in Flanagan's cell staring down at him sitting on the edge of his cot.

"So you didn't rob Wells Fargo," said Raider.

One of the deputies laughed. "I suppose Santa Claus give you that for Christmas."

"You're loco, Mr. Pink. You're all loco!" Flanagan switched his glare from one to another in turn. "I never been inside no Wells Fargo office in my life!"

"Your kid brother was accidentally killed on the job up in Dayton, Ohio," said Raider.

"So?"

"The job being Wells Fargo. The company felt sorry, they offered you money . . ."

"They felt shit!"

"You took their money, then you started taking your revenge, figuring on wiping out the whole operation, manager by manager. We got the notes you left, we got this money, the motive, the works."

Flanagan shifted his scowl from Raider to the sheriff. Small but well muscled through the chest and shoulders, Hazlett was a no-nonsense lawman. As cooperative as he could be in this case, acceding to every suggestion Raider proposed, every request. And he had about as much fondness for the prisoner as Flanagan had for Raider.

"It'll go one heck of a lot easier for you, brother, if you tell the truth and get it off'n your conscience," Hazlett said quietly.

"Fuck you, Mr. Hick badge! You bastards got no right to question me nohow anyways . . ."

Raider held up the money belt. "This is what's left of the Amarillo and the Wichita Falls jobs, isn't it."

"Balls! I got that money . . ." Flanagan paused. "None o' your goddamn business where I got it!"

Raider shrugged and handed the belt to Hazlett. "You'd best lock it up for me. It'll stand as material evidence. In time it'll be turned over to the law in Amarillo."

He got his receipt for the money belt and left the sheriff's office with Flanagan's curses ringing in his ears, adding to the lingering pain earlier inflicted by the big man's fists.

He checked into a room in the Sooner House Hotel, a box with an iron bed and a picture of a cow standing beside a barn decorating one wall. On the floor were two hemp carpets that had once been one hemp carpet, now ripped in half and placed on either side of the bed. According to the desk clerk this was "one of more desirable rooms in the entire hotel."

He slept until noon, the bed proving a good deal softer against shoulder blades, spine, and buttock bones than the frozen ground close by the Comanches' camp. At 12:30, after washing and redonning his unwashed denims, he got a corner table in the hotel dining room and proceeded to down two T-bone steaks half the size of his saddle. He then chased the lingering cold in his innards with better than a quarter of scalding hot coffee. Finally, feeling full, free-spirited, and frisky, he crossed the street to the Silver Bottle Bar and, edging up to the mahogany, ordered a bottle of bar whiskey and a glass.

"Make that two glasses, Mr. Small," said a musical female voice behind him.

He turned and gaped. She stood at least four full inches taller than he in her silver sequined high heels. Her hair was the color of fresh bran, long and curled at the ends. Her face was pretty, green eyes, a slender nose and a mouth, full and as inviting-looking as any Raider had ever kissed or put to other uses. What little God had given her in the way of breasts appeared to be afflicted with perpetual jiggle as she laughed.

"The name's O'Toole, lady."

"The name's Winifred, Winnie to you, O'Toole." She tossed her head back and laughed at nothing, jiggling her breasts and catching hold of the glass slid in her direction by the bartender. She set one hand atop Raider's bared head.

"I call most o' my men friends Mr. Small. No offense. I mean it ain't like you was Shorty Stallings. Do you know Shorty Stallings?"

He was about to answer but she wasn't about to let him. On she rambled. "He's about knee-high to a runty heifer and he swears he loves me six times more than his wife and his mother put together. Which is quite a sight. Both of 'em got faces like overworked choppin' blocks!"

"Hey, slow it down, big and busty."

She laughed and jiggled. The piano player switched from "My Mother's Heart" to "The Horse and the Whore," picking up the tempo. More and more customers were slamming in through the bat-wing doors as the afternoon wore on, and the sounds of gaiety and laughter and loud arguments mingled with the clinking of bottles and glasses.

"That's good," she said beaming. "Gettin' even, eh? Okay, I won't call you Mr. Small. You don't remind me I ain't exactly holdin' this rag up with the biggest cantaloupes in Cimarron County. You got good eyes?"

"Sure."

"How come you can't see my glass is empty?"

Raider grinned and poured. She was forward and looked a little like a beanpole in green satin, but he liked her. She was alive and cute as a damn kitten. She had personality and one helluva luscious-looking mouth. And in bed . . .

Half the bottle later that's where they were, stripped raw, naked as eggs, wrapped in each others arms, Raider feeling the warmth of her drawing the last of the winter cold out of the deepest, most remote recesses of his bones. Without his even realizing it, his cock had gotten as stiff as the pommel on a brand new saddle and twice as long, throbbing ready to plow the pole in his arms.

"O'Toole," she murmured, "that's Irish, ain't it?"

"So they tell me."

"I'm half Irish. The auld sod, my daddy used to call it. What say we talk about Ireland . . . . ?"

"Lady, I don't much want to talk about anything. Later, maybe, but at the moment . . ."

"You want to put that little old hard stove bolt into my fancy. You want to tickle my fancy."

"I'll give you more than a goddamn tickle," he said, insulted. "You can bet your auld sod on that!"

"Give me some and let's see . . ."

Uncurling her arms from around his back, she brought her hands down to her thighs and spread her lips. A whooshing sigh escaped Raider's lungs at sight of the object of his rapidly developing affection. She laughed merrily, jiggling everything; and in he went, all the way, every inch pulsing, throbbing, probing, driving against the wondrous, wide wet walls of Winnie's fancy.

"More! More!" she growled, her voice sensuous, her breath hot in his ear. She began nipping the lobe. "More . . ."

"That's it, lady."

"You're not serious!"

"So make more, dammit!"

"Hang on . . ."

She began gyrating, slowly at first, revolving her cunt around his cock, grating and grinding it, swelling it bigger, bigger . . . . No more banter now, no more laughing and witless giggling and nonsensical carrying on . . .

This was serious fucking, man and woman joined, one eight-limbed, two-headed, double-assed screwing machine, as Doc Weatherbee had so often, so poetically described it. She fucked with an intensity of purpose, a deliberation and determination that verged on the scary. She built his cock so big and so full so fast he envisioned

his balls, his thighs, every part of his body surrounding
stuffed into his cock and into her.

They drove and drove, one against the other. The bed
bounced and jounced, threatening to pound its way clear
through the floor, crashing walls and ceiling and half the
building down into the lobby below.

They came simultaneously, Raider's cares and concerns,
worries and woes, black memories and red head pain
vanishing in the load of come escaping his balls, surging
up his cock and into her fancy. . . .

They had started getting at each other in the middle
of the afternoon; they were still in the bed and at it four
hours later, fucking, sucking, and generally carrying on,
joining their short hairs in ways and positions Raider had
never imagined possible when, in the midst of a seemingly
hopeless effort on her part to reinstall stiffness into his
overworked cock, a gentle knock sounded at the door.

"Mr. O'Toole?"

Raider groaned, rolled over onto his stomach, with-
drawing his cock from her hard-working hand and burying his face in the pillow. "Go away . . ."

"Telegram for you, sir."

"Slip it under the door."

A yellow rectangle slid across the bare floor coming to
rest six inches from the end of the bed. Raider rolled
over onto his back, grabbing her wrist and restoring her
hand to his cock.

"Ain't you gonna read it?" she asked, her eyes brimming curiosity.

"Later. Tighter and faster, please."

"You oughta read it. It could be somebody died.
Some relative . . ."

"All I got is my aunt and uncle up in Butte, Montana
Territory. They're healthier than two twelve-year-olds."

Letting go of his cock, she leaned over the end of the
bed, displaying her pink cheeks to his admiring eyes,
and picked up the telegram.

"Let me open it for you?"

He shrugged. She tore open the envelope and eyed
the message with a look of rapidly growing bewilderment.

"What's it say?"

"It's some kinda foreign language."

Instantly he was wrenched back to reality, to business

and the importance of yellow envelopes and their contents. Bolting upright, he snatched it from her.

"Oh boy . . ."

"Can you read it? What's it say? Is it bad news? Did somebody die?"

"Do me a favor, go downstairs to the lobby and get me a pencil and paper."

"Let me get my dress and shoes on."

"The hell with your dress and shoes!"

"For God's sakes, I can't go down there mother-naked!"

"Yell down the stairs for the kid to bring 'em up. Hurry it up, please."

It wasn't good news; it wasn't "Investigation completed here. Nothing further to add. Nothing out of the ordinary." Raider had a special instinct regarding Doc's telegrams. Having worked together as long as they had, he could sense the contents of his partner's messages without even beginning to decode.

And what he sensed about this one set his heart pounding and his throat drying up quicker than a dead toad under a Mexican sun. One of any two people working together has to be the worry wart.

Why in hell, he wondered, did it have to be him?

18

The message from Doc did not decode into bad news. Disastrous would have been a more accurate adjective. Reading it over all but caused Raider to break into a sweat. He dismissed Winnie with a good-bye kiss, a promise to see her later, three dollars in cash, all that remained of the whiskey, and an explanation that his Aunt Bertha up in Butte was "down with pneumonia and not expected to survive the weekend."

Winnie dressed and, all sympathy and understanding, tucked the three dollars between the little protruberances crowning her chest and waved farewell with the bottle.

To make certain he had decoded Doc's message accurately, Raider repeated the entire tedious process letter by letter.

A third decapitation had taken place, this one in Clayton in northeastern New Mexico, nearly 400 miles from Wichita Falls. It had happened the night before, the night Raider had spent the better part of escorting Lock Flanagan to Boise City and the cell he was presently occupying.

Raider's eyes drifted to the cow standing beside the barn in the framed painting. "Bossy, I got the wrong man."

No anvil, not even a ninety-pound English tool steel job could have hit him harder. Or hurt more. The business about Flanagan's kid brother being accidentally killed, the notes left at the scenes, the $100,000 in the money belt, all the snugly fitting pieces suddenly didn't fit worth a damn. Lock Flanagan was as innocent as Winnie Whatever-her-name-was! How and where the big man had come by his fortune amounted to none of Raider's business. Or Doc's. Or Wells Fargo's. Or anybody's, except whoever he'd stolen it from . . .

Raider's next move was clear. Again he addressed the cow in the picture.

"I'll have to apologize to the son of a bitch and let him go. And buy him a new goddamn horse, too. Jesus Christ, I can't believe it!"

Nor could Sheriff Barney Hazlett or any of his deputies. The sheriff took his key ring down from the peg above his newly purchased flat-top, six-drawer desk and unlocked Flangan's cell door, swinging it wide.

"You're free to leave," said Hazlett, a trace of bitterness in his tone.

Raider, standing beside the sheriff, nodded. "I made a mistake, Flanagan. I apologize."

"Oh Jesus, that makes everything okay, don't it!" Flanagan bristled. "You cut your way into a man's home in the dead o' night, practically tear him outta his wife's arms, bind and gag her, hog-tie him, run him fifty miles through the coldest goddamn night o' the year, shoot his fuckin' horse dead . . ." He paused. "You owe me a horse!"

"You'll get it."

Flanagan's lip curled and he smirked. "I don't want just any horse. I want *a* partik'ler horse." He jabbed Raider's chest with his finger. "That little bay o' yours."

"You can't have it."

"You owe me, you Pink bastard."

"You want to start something up, Flanagan?" asked Hazlett acidly. "I can lock you up for disturbing the dang peace, you know. You ask for it, mister, you'll get it!"

"You shut up and get me my money belt, Mr. Sheriff Hick badge. And make sure every goddamn dollar's there!" Hazlett glanced at Raider.

"Give him his belt." He studied Flanagan. "That bay of mine would never be able to carry a man your size and you know it."

"You mean a man-sized man, ain't that what you mean?"

"You'd ride it to kill it, just to get even with me. I know goddamn well you would. I'll buy you a stallion, same size, same breed, same quality you had. You'll have to be satisfied with that."

Flanagan ran a forefinger up one bar and down the one next to it, nodding his head slowly in silence.

"Shit, Pink, I ain't no vindictive man what wants to hold no grudge. You got shit all over your face and burnin' into your eyeballs for this business. You're gonna have to answer to Wells and to Fargo and sixteen other guys before anybody lets you forget how you screwed up this one. Just gimme what I got comin' and I'm willin' to call it square." He extended his hand and grinned.

Raider shook hands with him. "I'm sorry. I fucked up, I admit it. I'll do what I can, everything I can to make things right."

"So what are we standin' here jawin' for? Let's get at it!"

19

Where Flanagan had come by his belt full of green-backs was a matter of intense curiosity to Sheriff Barney Hazlett. But Raider suddenly had too much else on his mind to worry about the where and the how of that. Just as long as it wasn't Wells Fargo's money. And there wasn't a sliver of proof that it was.

Gritting his teeth and downing his pride, Raider bought Flanagan a horse and a cosmoline new Colt .45 with money forwarded from the home office in Chicago. With the money had come a terse demand for a fuller explanation than Raider had provided in his hastily scribbled request handed to the Western Union clerk earlier that same day.

Flanagan rode away with a wave, laughing loudly, heading east for the Comanche camp. Standing on the front step of Hazlett's office watching the figure of the big man become smaller and smaller, Raider had a sudden suspicion that he would be waking up many a future night hearing that laugh, seeing that smirk, and recalling the dangerous and difficult time he had had bringing Flanagan to justice.

Justice. That would have been funny, had it not been so tragic. Was there such a thing?

In response to a second telegram from Doc requesting a rendezvous in Clayton, Raider set out at sunrise the following day following an enjoyable night with Winnie.

The day was the second of February, the morning unusually mild for the time of year in this part of the country. Most of the snow had melted, streams and rivers were giving indication of breaking up, and the sun showed a deeper color than any of the thirty-one January suns preceding it. It warmed the back of Raider's neck and the bay's flanks as they rode along at a leisurely pace. Clayton lay only fifty miles due southwest ahead—less than half a day's ride if he chose to push the horse. He'd rather not. He had cut its intended week-long rest period short by four full days; the least he could do was give it and himself the laziest, easiest ride possible over the border and into New Mexico. Once arrived, he would have to wait a week or more for Judith to haul Doc up from Wichita Falls. Besides, the health of the third victim in the Case of the Headless Wells Fargo Managers could scarcely deteriorate further if he, Raider, failed to reach Clayton before noon.

It would be good to see Doc again, he thought, although he'd be in for a merciless needling. Still, neither of them was responsible for the Flanagan blunder. Allan Pinkerton had gotten his direction from Wells Fargo; Raider and Weatherbee had only carried out wired orders.

He crossed the North Canadian River and passed a stage bound for Felt. He reined up by a stand of naked cottonwoods to rest the horse, dismounted, stretched his legs, and watched the stage pass by, the driver and shotgun waving. After unsaddling the bay, he let it wander while he set his saddle against a tree, unrolling his blanket to keep the ground chill from penetrating his bones. Then he tied the horse and lay down, the nape of his neck against the saddle. He dozed . . .

Raider was awakened what seemed like only seconds later, to a sight that chilled him faster and colder than the ground ever could. Drawn up in a semicircle in front of him were a dozen Comanche braves. And standing in front of them, the toes of her boots inches away from Raider's heels, was Flanagan's squaw.

20

If the most gifted sculptor in history had wished to fashion a female face that perfectly depicted pure hatred, he could have chosen for his model the girl staring down at Raider. In her right hand was a willow switch. Bringing it down sharply, she opened his face from cheek to jaw. His left hand went for his gun, his fingers slipping into the empty holster.

The girl hissed an order. A brave, taller than the others, with a knife-wound scar separating his lower lip from his chin like a band of white war paint, stepped forward.

"Stand up!"

Raider obeyed, bringing his hand down from his cheek, finding his fingers streaked with blood.

"Little Feather ask Pale-eyes where Flanagan hanged. Squaw want body . . ."

"Tell her he's not dead. He's got a horse, he's armed, he's on his way back to your camp."

The brave conveyed this to the girl. Her response was like venom escaping a rattler's mouth. She shifted hands, and up came the willow switch a second time. Raider caught her wrist, ripping the switch from her and tossing it away. The group started forward as one man. With hands raised, she stopped them.

The brave spoke. "Little Feather say you lie like all Pale-eyes. We come from camp. We not pass Flanagan."

"You missed him. You must have passed by Boise City before he pulled out."

No, reflected Raider immediately. That didn't make any sense. All it did was confuse Little Feather's interpreter, his bronzed brow crinkling. Then anger seized his features. She was rattling instructions at him, pointing at Raider, occasionally addressing the entire group.

"Little Feather say if husband alive, which jail?"

113

"Tell her he *was* in Boise City. That part's true. But the sheriff let him go. We had to. It was all a mistake. I made a mistake. Flanagan's not the man I'm looking for. . . ."

Little Feather spat out orders, her words coming so fast there seemed to be no break for syllables. But her interpreter had no difficulty understanding.

"He's on his way back to camp," repeated Raider. "I swear. You ride back, you'll see. He'll be there waiting. Tell her, for chrissakes!"

The interpreter was suddenly as heedless as a dynamite-deafened ore-cart jackass.

"We bring *you* back to camp."

Raider groaned aloud. Six little words that added up to a death sentence. He'd never see their camp alive, that he was certain. He'd heard too often how Comanches brought prisoners in, in their idea of sporting fashion. First they'd strip him naked, tie his wrists, and pony-drag him through all the snow they could find, and over all the sharp rocks between patches. If, by some singular act of God, he arrived at the camp still breathing, they would turn the squaws loose on him with willow switches and beat him to death—leaving him looking more like a pile of fresh buffalo meat than a man. And feeding his corpse to the camp dogs.

The interpreter stepped back and snapped at the two braves standing on either side of Little Feather. They came forward and were preparing to rip Raider's clothes from his body when the sound of galloping hooves was heard coming from the east. The braves had Raider's hat and jacket off and were working on his shirt when everything stopped, everyone froze, all eyes drifting in the direction of the oncoming sound.

Flanagan came pounding up on his new stallion, swinging to the ground even before the beast was fully halted. Screaming ecstatically, Little Feather ran to his arms. He picked her up like a child, lifting her high in the air, bringing her down, smothering her with kisses.

Never in his life had Raider been so relived to see anybody, friend or enemy. The conversation that followed the lovers' reunion established that Flanagan had indeed started out for camp. He had gotten halfway there, met one of Blue Wolf's braves, had been told that his squaw was on her way to Boise City after him, and had turned around and retraced his tracks. Riding back through Boise City, he'd easily picked up the Comanches' trail.

"Just in time, goddammit!" exclaimed Raider, striving for the friendliest tone of voice he could command. He redonned his jacket and restored his Stetson to his head, bringing a small spasm of pain to each side.

His neighborly reaction to Flanagan's appearance was regretfully based on an ill-founded assumption. The icy look in the big man's eyes confirmed it. He, Raider, had given Flanagan a hard night, winding it up killing the man's favorite horse. Sure, he'd eventually admitted he'd taken the wrong man, had apologized, made amends, done everything he could do, under the unwieldy and decidedly embarrassing circumstances.

But suddenly their positions were reversed. Flanagan held the hook and he, Raider, was on it.

The situation called for bluff, hope, luck, possibly even a quietly murmured prayer.

He extended his hand to Flanagan. "Funny, isn't it," he said.

"What?" asked Flanagan, ignoring the gesture.

"You asked to shake my hand, now I'm asking to shake yours. And hell, we didn't even know each other a couple days back."

"I didn't exactly ask to meet you, Mr. Pink," said Flanagan evenly, running the tip of his tongue over his upper lip and grinning frigidly. "You could even say you forced your way into makin' my . . . what you call it . . ."

"Acquaintanceship. Yeah, that's a fact. But I admitted I made a mistake."

"You didn't have much fuckin' choice, Mr. Pink."

"I'm not asking any favors. Just let me mount up and be on my way."

Flanagan began spouting Comanche, with admirable fluency, Raider noticed. All the braves roared with laughter. Little Feather didn't even smile. Now that he thought about it, Raider couldn't recall her taking her eyes off him for as long as three seconds since she and her braves had interrupted his nap.

Flanagan stared. "Did I hear you rightly? Did I hear you say you're *not* askin' any favors?"

"Just to leave."

"You askin' or beggin'?"

"Flanagan . . ."

"Mister Flanagan." Flanagan shook his head. "You're gettin' me all confused. I mean, what makes you so sure any of us wants you to leave?" His huge hand swept down the line of warriors. "These boys and my little girl has took a likin' to you, Mr. Pink. In fact, we like you so much, we're hereby invitin' you back to the camp. To join us for a little spree."

"I got business in New Mexico. . . ."

"It can wait, can't it?"

"Not really."

"Oh, sure it can. Business can allus wait. Just for, say, four or five days."

Raider pulled his hand down his injured cheek. The blood was beginning to clot, the wound closing, but it would show a scar for a long time. Maybe for as long as he lived.

"What's on your mind, Flanagan?" he asked coldly.

"Mister Flanagan."

"Mister . . ."

"Some sportin' fun. You and me facin' each other down in a Comanche ritchal series. No gamblin' or penny-ante horseshit, I'm talkin' about man-to-man doin's. Wrestlin' bareass in icy water, runnin' a switch gauntlet, knife duelin' with ankles hobbled and the ropes joined in the middle by a two-foot length o' sinew, the point bed."

"What in hell is that?"

"The boys take about forty two-foot stakes, sharpened at one end and jabbed into the ground points up. Formin' like a bed. I lays down on it and you piles rocks on me. The idee is to weight me down till it hurts so I yell quit. Then I do the same to you. The man which can hold up the fewest rocks loses.

"Oh, Mr. Pink, we got lotsa sportin' games. Ever see the way some o' the northern tribes stab hooks into a brave's chest just to see how long he can hang without screamin' to be let down or rippin' loose? Well, that there's the penalty the loser pays in our little Comanche ritchal' series."

He droned on and on. But nothing he added surprised Raider. Early in the conversation he had figured out the real reason for the competition. It was to be Flanagan's big chance to show off in front of Blue Wolf and the tribe. Show his squaw how strong and brave he was, how much stronger and braver than the puny little Pinkerton man.

There was one consolation, reflected Raider. At least they wouldn't be pony-dragging him back mother-naked over the freezing skin of No Man's Land.

They couldn't do that and arrive in camp with the co-star in shape for the big show.

21

Flanagan personally did the honors for the ride back, looping Raider's own lariat around his neck, running it down his spine, and tying his hands behind his back. The running length was pulled so tight, the rope around Raider's neck jerked his head back so that all he could see was sky, and pulled his wrists halfway up his back.

The party shunned the road, taking advantage of woodland cover and stretching single file down dried creek beds rapidly becoming barren of snow, taking every precaution to avoid meeting anyone, white or red.

Less than two miles along the way Raider's head began to feel as if at any moment it would snap off.

"Is that there rope a mite too tight?" asked Flanagan, riding alongside him. "If it is, I'd be more than happy to loosen her up. Too tight?"

"Nope."

"It looks tight. You sure?"

"Flanagan, you're a sadistic fucking bastard, you know that?"

Flanagan voiced no response. Instead he slapped Raider's horse hard across the rump with the flat of his hand, sending it lunging forward over the rough shale-littered ground, bouncing its rider, jerking the rope, the loop at Raider's throat cutting into his Adam's apple like a knife thrust.

He nearly passed out from the pain, the gray sky in his eyes darkening, then slowly regaining its original color. It was getting colder, the wind whipping down from the heights of Black Mesa behind them to the northwest across the Cimarron River.

A mile later Flanagan, who had dropped back to ride with Little Feather, came galloping up, knife in hand, and with a single swipe parted the rope joining Raider's neck to his wrists, instantly relieving the pressure and the pain.

"My little girl says you got to be in shape when we gets home," Flanagan said leering. "I'm only tellin' you that on account I wouldn't want you thinkin' I was goin' soft or nothin'."

"Yeah."

Uttering the single word seemed to swell Raider's apple to twice its normal size in his throat. Jesus Christ, he probably wouldn't be able to swallow anything but buffalo blood soup for a week! Which didn't matter all that much, figuring he likely wouldn't last two days, let alone seven.

"One other thing, Mr. Pink, don't go tryin' to get away like I tried the other night. I'll kill your bay *and* you." The tell-tale click of cocking sounded in Raider's right ear. "With your own goddamn Winchester."

Strong Bow, Little Feather's interpreter and, according to Flanagan, also Blue Wolf's eldest son, led them through a series of depressions and arroyos, taking advantage of the concealment afforded by outcroppings, using every available natural cover to keep the party out of sight of anyone in or around Boise City. Raider wistfully hoped that Sheriff Barney Hazlett and his deputies might be out combing the area, looking for somebody's stolen cattle or missing prize mustang. But they saw no one.

With Boise City somewhere off the point of Raider's left shoulder and, he guessed, something close to forty miles separating them from the camp, it began to snow, flat flakes half the size of poker chips settling slowly to earth. No blizzard, and even if one were waiting inside the now sunless slate sky overhead it would not arrive before the Comanches' tepees came into view.

On and on they rode, seeing no living creature, not so much as a wandering prairie wolf. They reached the banks of the North Canadian and were preparing to cross the rope and plank bridge slung over its ice-encrusted surface when the brave riding point some fifty yards ahead came galloping back jabbering loudly, flinging his arms and pointing in the direction of the higher land crowning the opposite side of the river. The party stopped and Strong Bow came riding back to Flanagan, Little Feather, and Raider and two young braves riding as a group.

There was more palaver, which quickly developed into an argument soon settled by Strong Bow. He turned to Flanagan, and the big man nodded agreement.

"What have we got up ahead?" asked Raider. "Some nice blue cavalry riding out of Willowbar looking for you?"

"You should be so lucky, Mr. Pink." Flanagan laughed, patting him on the back. "It's an Arapaho hunting party. Six lonesome braves with about eight tons o' meat, accordin' to the boy up front."

Strong Bow spoke to Flanagan, who relayed his words to Raider. "We're crossing over and goin' after their asses."

"Are you keeping me informed because you want my blessing?"

"I'm givin' you fair warnin'. This is gonna be quick an' easy, us fourteen against six stinkin' Dog Eaters.* It'll be all over in two minutes. Don't get any dumb idees. I'm keepin' one eye on you. . . ."

They rode out, clattering across the plank bridge and up the other side, Raider, Little Feather, and Flanagan bringing up the rear. The snow was coming down heavier now and as they gained the rise, reined up, and watched. The Comanches charged the hapless Arapahos, taking them almost completely by surprise. Raider's heart welled with pity for the six men escorting a string of twelve horses loaded down with buffalo meat in hide sacks. With bows and arrows and lances, the Comanches went at them with a savage fury that chilled Raider's marrow. Why waste precious ammunition on six practically powerless man-squaws? For these were obviously far from first-rate warriors; not one of the six had even a rusty Sharps.

The Comanches had lined up and let fly a volley of arrows, dropping four of the hunters. The other two rode off pursued by four braves wielding lances. They caught up with them easily and skewered them like boiled meat in a pot.

The victorious attackers gathered around the pack

---

* The Shoshones hated the Southern Arapahos and nicknamed them Dog Eaters. The Comanches were generally friends and allies of the Shoshones.

horses, a number of the Comanches dismounting, some to relieve the corpses of their scalps and knives and anything else worth looting. The entire savage sequence was all over in less than two minutes, by Raider's reckoning. All six Arapahos lay dead, scalped and left where they lay as the snowflakes settled on scattered patches of fresh blood, their crystalline beauty absorbing it.

The pack horses milled about in confusion as Strong Bow, his braves, and even Flanagan rode about admiring their catch, commenting, congratulating one another.

Raider was perplexed. Twelve horses, loaded with enough meat to feed the entire troop complement of Fort Sill for practically the entire winter, escorted by six lightly armed Arapahos. How, he asked himself, had so few hunters managed to bring down so many buffalo? Unless they'd found most or possibly even all of them frozen to death, the carcasses sufficiently thawed by the early morning sun to permit them to begin butchering. But . . .

All the questions rapidly rising to mind found a single answer in the next moment. Over a rise less than a hundred yards to the south came the sound of thunder preceding a horde of Arapahos, at least eighty fully armed hunters. They had spied the carnage wrought by the attacking Comanches and were riding into battle screaming fit to split the heavens!

Most of Strong Bow's men had dismounted and were busy either further mutilating the corpses or checking the loads of meat. The charging Arapahos were on them like a tidal wave sweeping over a rock, sending them scrambling like crabs. The sound of gunfire was deafening.

The Comanches dropped like apples from a tree. Caught unawares, unable to get his squaw out of the bloody arena, Flanagan attempted to shield her with his body, blasting away with Haber Selkirk's Winchester.

But a lone Arapaho came at him from his left side while he was engaged in cutting down two attacking from the right. A single shot from the Arapaho's rifle caught the big man squarely in the temple, felling him from his horse like a tree dropped.

Raider could hear Little Feather screaming; he did not see her. He saw only the bridge stretching invitingly in front of him. Thumping the bay with his heels, pounding as hard as he could, then hanging on with his thighs, he shot across, reacing the other side riding like the Black Mesa wind, the sounds of the slaughter at his back becoming fainter . . . fainter. . . .

22

Weaponless, his wrists still tied behind him, Raider rode southwest, gradually slowing the horse. He crossed the Texas border into Sherman County, intent on getting into Hartley and picking up the Dalhart-Ware road which would take him straight to Clayton.

That would most likely be the road Judith and her friend would be taking up from Amarillo. Coming from Wichita Falls as Doc was, Raider figured he would backtrack to Amarillo, the crossroads of northwestern Texas. And whether he came out of there on the Wildorado road or Pleasant Valley–Masterson northbound trail, sooner or later he too would reach Dalhart. From Dalhart to Clayton was an almost straight line roughly fifty miles long. Raider would be there days before Doc's wagon.

Spotting a ledge of sandstone as sharp-looking as a new stubble plow, he swung down and easily cut the ropes binding him, not a drop of blood accompanying their parting.

No doubt about it, this particular Pinkerton's luck was changing. Maybe he was getting some of Flanagan's, whatever was left over after the big man had stopped the Arapaho's bullet with his head. Now Little Feather, unblushing bride filled with love for her Lock and an equal amount of loathing for Raider, was a widow.

Or a corpse. No, she was much too comely to kill. Better to fetch her back into slavery or make her a pass-around pleasure toy for the younger bucks of the tribe. The dice shouldn't have come up snake-eyes. Strong Bow, with Flanagan's support, shouldn't even have tossed them. At first sight of those six Arapahos hauling all that meat home, Raider's suspicions had been aroused. But so eager to grab it and wipe out the despised Dog Eaters were Strong Bow and the rest, that nobody had bothered to take the time to weigh matters. No sir; just bull on in, kill, and grab. Now every blessed one, save possibly the girl, was lying in the snow, deader than the petrified pines out in the Navaho Four Corners Country.

The senseless bastards, one and all! He could just picture some cut-nose Arapaho parading around his camp waving Flanagan's $100,000 money belt—a battle trophy that didn't mean half as much to the victor as the Irishman's scalp drying in the Indian's lodge and soon to be proudly displayed from his belt.

Four days later, flat broke, hungry, minus all his weapons including his straight razor, tired and coming down with a cold, Raider stood beside his horse out of the wind near a boulder half the size of Boise City and watched a familiar mule pull an equally familiar-looking wagon slowly up the frozen rut-ravaged road toward Dalhart.

23

"You got anything back there for a cold?" asked Raider, striving for casualness in his tone, aware that confessing that his health was less than perfect to this particular Doc Weatherbee would be leaving himself wide open to a boring lecture, and all the censure Doc could heap upon his head.

Doc had greeted him as if he were a dead brother risen from the grave. The horse was tied onto the tailgate, Raider joined his partner on the driver's seat, and they exchanged their recent experiences as they passed through Dalhart, stopping long enough to eat, feed and water the animals, and purchase Raider a secondhand Remington .44 before continuing northward toward Clayton.

Doc reached behind him, fumbling in a carton and coming up with an unlabeled bottle. He handed it to Raider.

"Drink half now, half before you tuck in for the night, little fella."

"What is it?" asked Raider suspiciously.

"What's ailing you?"

"I already told you, a cold. Nothing big, just a sniffle." He sniffled and wiped his runny nose with the back of his gloved hand.

"So what do you think I'd give you, something for menstrual pain?"

"There's no goddamn label. For all I know it could be liquid rat poison!"

"You're a trusting soul, you know that, Rade?" Doc snorted and spat petulantly. "When you were a baby and you started talking, I'll bet your first words to your mother were, 'Are you my mother? Can you prove it?'"

"Oh shut up. You're about as funny as a knife in the brisket."

"Speaking of knives in the brisket, that's something I forgot to tell you."

"What?"

"First drink up . . ."

Raider drank. It tasted like gall but he managed to get it down without bringing it right back up. Recorking the bottle, he jammed it into his rear pocket, reserving his comments on the foul taste of the stuff.

The weather had warmed up again, the sky was cloudless and blue, and the mesquite and sagebrush scattered about the landscape here on the edge of the Staked Plains, despite their drab winter coloring, were a welcome sight. Even heading northward into colder country didn't bother Raider. He would have run up to Alaska in preference to chasing about No Man's Land, with its damn blizzards and Comanches and Arapahos and six-foot-seven-inch Irishmen who hurt people's heads with his fists.

Being reunited with Doc was even more welcome than the pleasant weather, the change in scenery and the serenity that came with it; though he'd rather sit down in a tub filled with tarantulas before admitting it.

"You were talking about a knife. . . ." Raider began.

"In the brisket, yes. That was one final touch to the murder down in Wichita Falls I neglected to tell you about. Remember my mentioning how nervous the murdered man's assistant was?"

"Hubert somebody . . ."

"Prtichard. Well, he hated Hubbell. Rade, I never knew how much one person could hate another until he admitted it." Raider scowled in confusion. "I don't mean he killed Hubbell."

"He was afraid you'd figure he did, though, considering the way the two of 'em got on. Is that it?"

Doc explained. Since the deceased was headless, the casket had been closed at the wake and at the funeral. But when Doc showed the standard permission form signed by Pauline Hubbell allowing him, in the company of Dr. Sligh and the undertaker, to open the grave, when the lid of the casket was lifted . . .

"Guess what?" asked Doc.

"Guess shit!"

"There was a damn knife sticking in Hubbell's heart.

Hubert Pritchard broke down and owned up. He hated Hubbell so much he'd sneaked into the funeral parlor, opened the lid of the casket, and shoved that knife into him."

"He was already dead." Raider stared. Grabbing Judith's reins out of Doc's hands, he whoaed her to a stop. "Is this another one of your jokes?"

"It's the God's honest truth. Cross my heart and hope to die!" Taking back the reins, he started Judith off. "Pritchard was just plain mad."

"Crazy . . ."

"Not crazy, sore as hell because Hubbell had gotten himself murdered before he, Pritchard, had a chance to get even with him for seventeen months of misery, insults, and humiliation. The man had to get in his own personal lick. When he confessed to me in the office, he broke down and cried like a baby. Then he stood up and began yelling, 'I'm glad I did it! I'd do it again!' "

"What did you do?"

Doc shrugged. "What could I do? I had to tell the marshal. Knowing all the facts, knowing Hubbell and Pritchard and their relationship, I suppose I could have kept mum. Except that Dr. Sligh and the undertaker saw the knife too."

"What do you think they'll do to Pritchard?"

"For killing a dead man?" Again Doc shrugged. "Nothing much. The man's wife's an invalid. He does a good job for Wells Fargo; Hubbell would have fired him long ago if he didn't. I don't think they'll do anything to him. Unless they decide to bring in an alienist and he finds he really is crazy. He's not, though." Doc paused and stared at the horizon. And shook his head. "He just hated. . . ."

Raider coughed and again wiped at his nose.

"Maybe you'd better finish that bottle right now," said Doc.

"No thanks, tonight'll do just fine."

24

Eighty thousand dollars missing. The identical murder method. The same note. Shortly after the two had arrived in Clayton and completed their preliminary examination of the office, Doc shooting photographs of everything in sight, he was summoned to the local Western Union office and advised to contact "a Mr. Wagner in Chicago at your earliest possible convenience."

They drove together out onto the Seneca road where Raider ran the wire up a telegraph pole, hooked Doc on, and returned to the wagon to sit and watch him call in.

The word from Wagner was clear and its content fully expected. In brief, his complaint involved their continuing failure to solve the case, to even unearth what might be considered any worthwhile clues—and Allan Pinkerton's rapidly increasing impatience with their lack of progress. The Agency's president and chief executive officer was known far and wide for his short fuse. The Wells Fargo people were hounding him. In Wagner's opinion this was not surprising; the company had already lost three office managers and close to $300,000. And the entire grisly and expensive business could conceivably go on "for the next ten years."

Doc decoded and read the unhappy news to Raider.

"He's dead wrong about that part," Raider commented.

"What part?"

"This thing going on ten years . . ."

"Whether it does or not, you and I are going to be pulled off it and shipped to Siberia if we don't start showing results goddamn soon!"

Raider shifted his weight from a crate of Cantwell's Consumption Cure to one containing seventy-two bottles of Dr. Squire's Quick Cure for Indigestion and Dyspepsia

—and started on his own third bottle of the bitter-tasting cold medicine prescribed by his partner.

"Something stinks," said Doc quietly. Raider sniffed. "About this case, you idiot! There's something very wrong, something crazy. But I'm damned if I can put my finger on it. Take the wire down; let's go back into town, sit down in the hotel room, and put our heads together."

"Okay."

Matters had reached the critical stage. Neither man could begin to bear the thought of being taken off the case. It was a matter of pride. It wasn't the blizzard and the Indians and the pains in his head and throat to Raider, nor the troublesome whores or the boring traveling about to Doc. It was the undigestible idea of letting down the Agency.

Sitting in the room in the Clayton Hotel that they would be sharing, they discussed every aspect of both previous cases and what they had learned about the present one.

The Clayton office manager's name was Peter Rankin. A widower like Sam Grater in the Amarillo office, Mr. Rankin had been with Wells Fargo for nineteen years. He had been a manager for ten. And his record for loyalty and devotion to the job was second to no man in the entire organization, according to the members of his staff.

Rankin's body was examined, identification confirmed by a close friend along with his employees, and was to be laid to rest the following morning, his interment delayed almost a week to accommodate relatives arriving from the north.

At six o'clock, their minds thoroughly staggered by their afternoon-long efforts to sift the available clues and consistencies relevant to the three cases, Raider and Doc repaired to The Silver Slipper down the street from the hotel.

The Slipper was a bar like a hundred others up and down the territories: the same stretch of gleaming, ring-stained mahogany; the identical mirror below a framed painting of a reclining nude overlooking legions of labeled and unlabeled bottles; the same sounds and smells and songs and sirens. Although both men drank, side by side in silence, neither had the slightest interest in beauty after beauty who approached them.

They ate supper. They returned to their room sober and crestfallen to the point of downright discouragement. The room was distinguished by filthy chintz curtains framing the dirty windows, bare walls painted inestimable years earlier a pale mausoleum granite color, a floor that appeared to have been diligently swept and mopped at least once every season, and two single brass beds, remarkably new-looking, dentless, and to the surprise of both, comfortable.

Exhausted by their mental labors, they fell asleep minutes apart. In the middle of the night Doc awoke with a start, sitting up in bed and yelling:

"I've got it! I've got it! I've got it!"

"For chrissakes," groaned Raider rolling over and struggling valiantly to get one eye open.

Doc was out of bed lighting the kerosene lamp sitting on the apple crate upended and in service as a table between the two beds.

"I've got it! I've got it! I've got it!"

"You'll get it, goddamnit, if you don't stop carrying on like a fuckin' Cheyenne medicine woman. And let me get some goddamn sleep!"

"Sleep your ass! Sit up. Put your feet on the floor. Listen, I've got it figured. . . ."

Raider yawned. "So tell me, only not so loud. Jesus Christ, you'll wake up the whole town!"

"The three murders aren't murders," announced Doc in a tone that suggested Moses preparing to introduce the Ten Commandments to his followers.

"Go back to sleep. . . ."

"I mean it, Rade. I'll bet you the world, the sky, and all the fucking stars all three of those bastards are as alive as you are. Alive, healthy, and working overtime defrauding the goddamn company!"

"How?"

Doc listed a number of what he insisted upon defining as facts, ticking them off on his fingers and stressing that although no single one of his "facts" could be considered particularly incriminating, taken together: "They're suspicious as hell."

He began by citing the knowledge that "if you don't

count Pauline Hubbell," none of the three left a family. And you didn't have to count her. If, he declared, Wilbur Hubbell loved old Pauline twice as much as she loved him, he'd leave her faster than a bullet leaves a Sharps. Any man married to her would walk, given the chance.

"I met her, I got to know her. You've got to take my word for it. Just bear with me, don't interrupt, let me get it all out before you start kicking the props out from under."

"I'm not saying a word."

Blood had been found spattered about all three offices, and yet none of the three so-called victims showed any blood on his clothing. In Doc's opinion this suggested that the corpses were placed *after* the "stage was set"—a consistent oversight on the part of whoever was masterminding the scheme.

"Why" he asked rhetorically, "the vanished heads in all three cases? Because absence of the heads would permit the mastermind to substitute a fresh corpse for the supposed corpse of the manager, a body resembling him physically, dressed in his clothing, wearing his jewelry . . . the works. Considering the shocking circumstances, who would think to question the dead man's identity?"

Before Raider could answer, on he went. Who but a former or present Wells Fargo employee would know enough about the case involving the late Lock Flanagan's younger brother to use it as the motive for the three "killings"?

Raider nodded. "Grater, Hubbell, and Rankin would know."

"Right!"

Doc's firmest conviction was that a fourth party was masterminding the crime spree, selecting the "victims," supplying the fresh corpses with suitable builds and weights, leaving the notes, helping the managers get away.

"Where to?"

Doc frowned. "You didn't have to ask that, Rade. That's *the* question. And there's no answer. Not yet."

"Which makes this whole powwow just one big fat theory."

"Is it a good one?" asked Doc. "Does it make sense?"

"Yeah . . ."

"You bet it does!"

Sitting back down on the edge of his bed, he leaned over and blew out the lamp.

"What are you doing?" asked Raider.

"Going back to sleep. Tomorrow we start work. Good night."

Raider leaned back on his pillow staring at the swipe of moonlight crossing the ceiling. "You know all that money could be going into one big pot, buying something, investing in something, swindling somebody . . . thousands making millions."

"Right. Good night."

"And if we locate one of the three, we'll find 'em all."

"Yeah. Good night."

"You and me can come out of this shining like a baby's ass!"

"Good night."

"We . . ."

"Good Night!"

25

Raider slept fitfully the remainder of the night while Doc snored away contentedly, his mind obviously at ease, the case solved. The more the restless Raider thought about it, the more sense Doc's idea seemed to make. All three corpses without so much as one drop of blood on their shirts or shoulders was the key.

Doc snored on, so loudly the sound practically shifted the position of his bed.

Dawn, gray but snowless, was filtering through the curtains when Raider was finally able to turn his mind off completely and fall into deep sleep. Moments later, a bright-eyed, well-rested, chippery Doc was shaking him awake, practically pulling him out of bed.

"Let's get at it!"

"I'll be right with you," murmured Raider thickly. "Give me an hour. . . ."

"Up!"

"One stinking hour . . ."

"Up!"

They washed up and dressed in under two minutes, postponing shaving and breakfast, hurrying to the stable, rousing the sleeping man in charge, and half an hour later they were back at the same pole on the Seneca road hooking up and calling the Chicago office.

It promised a lovely day, windy, an icy chill in the air, the sky a miserable gray that by comparison made the walls of their hotel room look cheerful. But a lovely day, nevertheless. Turning the big corner in a case always made the day a diamond.

All they needed now was Wagner's go-ahead. It wouldn't come easily or speedily. Even if he liked the idea, he'd have to consult with Allan Pinkerton and others in the office. They would sit around the conference table and pick the thing to pieces like a pack of famished coyotes going after a buffalo calf.

Both men sat in the wagon hovering over the transmitter as Doc waited patiently between efforts to get through.

"We're crazy!" snapped Raider. "They'll piss all over it. They'll block us before we even get started."

"You're jumping to conclusions."

"I'm not jumping to anything! It's the way it'll turn out and you know it. I say fuck calling in. Let's just get to work. I figured it all out while you were asleep."

"Did you really?"

"Wiseass. . . . Seriously, we check out all three corpses. Dig 'em up and have somebody examine 'em, every inch inside and out.

"There have to be clues . . . something."

"Why don't we rent us some shovels and dig 'em up ourselves? Make it easy for us," said Doc, his tongue pushing out his cheek.

"We could get into a lot of trouble doing that."

"Rade, face it, get it into your head and keep it there. We have got to get off right. Which means "Okay—go ahead" from Chicago."

"What if they turn us down? Next thing you know we're pulled off the goddamn case and sent up to Des Moines or Sioux City to find some son of a bitch's lost cat! Or maybe even fired. Three bucks a day isn't exactly hen feed. I've worked my ass off on this thing. . . ."

"Oh, shut up!"

Doc's sounder clicked to life. Throughout the next three hours messages were encoded, tapped out, received, decoded until after what seemed more like three years orders came through to, as Wagner phrased it "Pursue your own initiatives regarding Case No. 3189."

Weekly reports would have to be filed, complete explanations of the team's activities and progress. This and the customary caution to keep expenses down were the only strings attached.

Doc clicked off with a flourish and joined Raider in a wolf howl of triumph, startling Judith and Raider's horse so they all but left the ground.

26

They returned to Amarillo accompanied by a coffin containing the mortal remains of the gentleman found in front of the blown safe in the Clayton Wells Fargo office. Upon arrival in Amarillo, Doc engaged the services of a former coroner, one Dr. Ezekiel Fellstone who, from his manner, his sepulchral tone of voice and dour appearance, impressed Raider as having spent too much time with dead people and not nearly enough with living ones. But he was a man whose skills were accorded the highest regard by his fellow physicians in the area.

The second corpse, the one used to replace Sam Grater, was disinterred and brought to Fellstone for examination. Doc then stabled Judith and his wagon, rented a team and buckboard, and fairly flew the more than two hundred miles to Wichita Falls to get the body substituted for Wilbur Hubbell's.

He met with Dr. Sligh in the doctor's office after hours and explained the situation in detail. Sligh was in his seventies, but as bright-eyed and sharp-minded as a man half his years. He clearly understood Doc's need, but hesitated to offer his cooperation.

"Have you spoken with Pauline yet?"

"No, sir. I'm not about to stick my hand into that mess of snakes."

"She is a pure delight, I agree." Sligh put his fingers to his lips as if to stop his mouth and walked to the window to look down upon the street. The scent of antiseptic teased Doc's nostrils as he glanced about the modest little office at the twin bookcases, the small flat-topped rock maple desk and chair beneath Sligh's framed medical school diploma, and the door to the examining room, three inches ajar.

Then his eyes wandered to the vested back of the slender, narrow-shouldered man looking down upon Wichita

Falls and all too obviously wrestling with his conscience.
At length Sligh turned and peered at him over the tops of
his spectacles.

"Still, Pauline is Wilbur's wife. And exhuming the
corpse a second time . . ."

"We didn't 'exhume' it the first."

"You know what I'm saying."

"Doctor, that corpse is not Wilbur Hubbell's."

"So you say. Your people agree with you. Wells Fargo
agrees with you."

"You don't?"

"I do. . . ."

"Then what's the problem?"

"The problem is that if you follow this business through
to completion and find you're wrong, that it was nothing
more than an ingenious idea—son, you're going to have
your hands mighty full. Pauline Hubbell will march to the
nearest lawyer and institute suit against you and your
partner and the Pinkertons and Wells Fargo and seventy-
three others demanding nine times ten million dollars."

"My mistake," said Doc soberly. "I thought we had covered all that."

Sligh studied him with a look that blended sympathy
and concern in equivalent amounts.

"Wouldn't the most sensible thing be to bypass Pauline?
Simply not let her know we're disinterring the body?" persisted Doc.

"I don't know as you can bypass her, legally. I'm no
lawyer, but until you can prove otherwise, that corpse out
in Pleasant Glade cemetery is Wilbur Hubbell's."

"You know goddamn well it's not," said Doc deliberately but without rancor in his tone.

Sligh nevertheless raised his hands defensively. "Easy.
I'm on your side, remember? But I've got to live in this
town. If I'm party to something that that blows up in all
our faces, it could wreck my practice. Paint my reputation
blacker than the inside of your hat on your head."

Doc thought a moment. Then he brightened. "What if
I didn't come here today?"

"You mean what if you're not here now? What if I
haven't seen you since back then . . . ?"

"Exactly!"

"Good-bye. Good luck."

27

A distant owl hooted disapprovingly, the wind softly flapped the front of Doc's covert box mackintosh, and the slice of ice that was representing itself as the quarter moon slipped behind a cloud shaped like a badly crushed pillow. The darkness deepened over the open grave, and the team between the shafts of the buckboard stirred uneasily.

The cemetery caretaker rested on his shovel, his eyes darting about uneasily. His necessary presence had set Doc back fifty dollars, a fortune that would be impossible to explain on his expense account. Allan Pinkerton himself went over every operative's expense account with a slow, well-practiced eye. Three cents invested in a plug of Boot Jack Tobacco that accidentally found its way into an operative's account sheet unaccompanied by a thorough and fully acceptable explanation would be redlined quicker than pickpocket's hand.

Fifty dollars' bribe money to dig up a corpse and replace it with rocks . . . Doc refused to think further about it. At least at the moment. His shovel, thrust downward, hit wood.

"That's it," whispered the caretaker, a fat, sweaty individual as nervous, at least at the moment, as Doc had ever seen Hubert Pritchard.

"Are you going to stand there watching me all night or are you going to help?" asked Doc.

"You didn't ask me to help, friend. That little contribution you give me was supposed to be for my permission."

"That little contribution is a fairly goddamn big contribution, 'friend.' The least you could do is lend a hand clearing the lid. Between us we can get it up and onto the wagon."

"That we could."

"Okay, then . . ."

"Cost you twenty-five bucks more."

"Jesus Christ!"

"Cheap. I could lose my job if anybody spots us." For about the thirtieth time since the ghoulish proceedings had gotten under way, the man glanced about nervously.

"Shit! What in hell do you want with a caretaker's job anyway? You could make a million blackmailing people. You've got talent."

"No call to get snotty-tongued . . ."

Doc had never heard the phrase before. The two words combined struck him as disgusting. As did his unhelpful helper. Muttering further insults under his breath, he got out his billfold, counted out twenty-five additional dollars, and handed them to the man.

"Thank you kindly. You're a charitable gent, I must say."

"Either that or a goddamn sucker. Let's go, let's fin- ish. . . ."

Getting the casket up and into the buckboard nearly gave Doc a hernia. Why Wilbur Hubbell's stand-in hadn't been buried in a plain pine coffin struck him as the mys- tery of the decade—knowing how Pauline felt about her husband. But this damnable two-ton-what-lifted-like- mostly-lead casket introduced by the overblown, tin- earred, tea-swilling bitch for appearances' sake alone could, reflected Doc, easily cripple him for life.

Somehow between the two of them they completed the job, filling the grave with the rocks, shoveling back the dirt, and carefully replacing the sod atop it.

"Christ Almighty," moaned the caretaker rubbing one hand down the inside of his thigh. "I think I pulled a milk muscle."

"Good," said Doc, climbing onto the driver's seat and flicking the reins, starting the horses down the hill to the gate and the road leading left back into Wichita Falls.

And right to Iowa Park and eventually Amarillo.

28

In Doc's absence from Amarillo, Raider pored over the journals of all three cases and had two hundred copies each made of Grater's, Hubbell's, and Rankin's photographs. At the proper time these would be circulated and more copies made and sent out until the entire country was blanketed.

The three corpses lay side by side on their chests on adjacent tables in Dr. Fellstone's examining room. The room itself was similar in layout to the preparation room in Sessions Funeral Parlor on the other side of town. But the cabinets lining these walls displayed a larger and wider variety of surgical instruments with less space devoted to cosmetic supplies.

Doc joined Fellstone. Raider had been invited to do so, but had declined, electing to await the outcome of the autopsies in the bar across the street.

"Isn't your partner interested in this aspect of the case?" inquired Fellstone, standing at his wash basin lathering, scrubbing, and rinsing his hands.

"He doesn't much like cadavers," replied Doc.

Fellstone snickered. "He doesn't know what he's missing. The trained eye can see more in a dead body than the living patient can possibly tell his doctor. Or, for that matter, the doctor can ascertain for himself. I'll make no bones about it, Mr. Weatherbee, I find my work fascinating." Drying his hands, he went to the nearest cabinet and selected a number of scalpels and other instruments. He arranged them on a metal tray and brought the tray to the first table. Upon it lay Wilbur Hubbell's substitute.

Fellstone had already completed his external examinations of the three bodies. As he had informed both Doc and Raider even before removing the clothing, there would be little hope of finding anything as helpful as a tattoo, or anything else unusual, on any of the three.

"If your theory is correct," he had said to Doc, "whoever is behind this business must have been extremely careful in selecting his bodies."

"So you didn't find anything," said Doc in a disconsolate tone, picking up the thread of their previous conversation.

"I didn't say that," said Fellstone.

"Is there anything in common, anything at all?"

The coroner nodded. "See for yourself." He drew two fingers down the nearest corpse's spinal column. "Run your fingers down all three spines the same way."

Doc did so. "They're not exactly straight as a string."

"Few people's are, but these are badly out of line. These men must have done heavy work; their hands don't show it as much as their backs. Probably because they wore gloves on the job. But whatever that job was, it was hard labor."

"Managing a Wells Fargo office isn't exactly lifting and lugging, like a stevedore or construction worker."

"And very few people go from one line into another so entirely different."

Doc nodded agreement, smiling inwardly. Fellstone appeared to enjoy playing detective as much as he enjoyed his work.

"There's one other external indication," continued Fellstone. He motioned Doc to Wilbur Hubbell's substitute and pointed to a scar in the right buttock, almost in the center of it.

"It looks like a bullet hole."

Fellstone concurred. "Old wound, very old. You can tell from the condition of the scar tissue. Now I'm going to open them up. Hopefully we'll do as well inside as out. Have you ever been present at an autopsy before?"

"No."

"Then I'd suggest you join your partner across the street. I'll send a boy over for you."

"When do you think?" Doc took out his Commander Elgin watch. "It's five to one."

"I'll need at least four hours to do a thorough job."

"That's what we need."

They sat at a table in the back room of the bar across the street from Fellstone's, a bottle of Valley Tan between them. They examined and reexamined the journals the first hour, then getting a pack of cards from the man who brought them their second bottle of whiskey, attempted to pass the remaining three hours playing two-handed stud. Neither one was really interested in the game. They were too wound up with hope and anticipation, and fidgety with impatience.

"It's working, isn't it?" said Raider in a prayerful tone. "Say it is."

"It looks to be, Rade. Who knows? We still have a long road ahead." Slamming down a jack, he seized the cards from Raider's hand and began collecting the deck.

"What are you doing?"

"You don't want to play, I don't want to play. Not two-handed stud." Squaring the deck, Doc shuffled and started laying out solitaire.

"Maybe I'd like to play fuckin' solitaire!" Raider snapped.

"I doubt you know how."

"You're an insulting bastard, you know that?"

"Drink your drink. And pour me some more."

"Pour your own!"

"What are you so edgy about?"

"What are you? What are you putting a black queen on a black king for?"

Doc corrected the mistake. "You know, I really could have used your strong back and weak mind down in Wichita Falls. That caretaker was about as much help as the corpse!"

Raider quietly disclosed that, like morgues and funeral parlor preparation rooms, cemeteries after dark were not to his liking. They talked, they argued. They drank and checked the time by Doc's Elgin again and again. Doc failed to go out in his one-man game twenty-three times running and finally tossed the deck to Raider in disgust.

"What time is it?" Raider asked.

"I just told you thirty seconds ago."

"A minute, at least . . . more."

Doc reacted in exasperation and went for his watch. A timid knock sounded.

"Mr. Weatherbee?"

Raider opened the door to a small boy with a face

littered with freckles, a grin lacking two front teeth, and his cap squeezed into a lump between his hands.

"Doc Fellstone says to come on over right away. Quick!"

Out they rushed, leaving the journals, the scattered cards, the all but empty bottle, and the boy in their wake, his grin replaced by bewilderment. They ran so fast out the swinging doors, across the street, and into Fellstone's office, that Raider almost ran into the room occupied by the three cadavers. Catching himself at the door just in time, he squeezed both eyes shut, spun about, and fairly threw himself into the waiting room.

Fellstone was drying his hands, his face as sober as a death mask, as usual. He was talking to himself, nodding in agreement with himself, when Doc cleared his throat to announce his presence. The three corpses were each concealed under a freshly laundered sheet.

Fellstone greeted them, then, holding up one finger for patience, picked up a yellow writing pad, lifted the top sheet filled with scribbling, and examined the one under it.

"What is it? What'd you find?"

"You'll never be able to read my writing."

"So tell me!"

"Sit." Fellstone pulled up chairs for them and they sat. By this time Doc was exerting every ounce of will power to restrain himself from grabbing Fellstone by the arms and shaking it out of him.

Fellstone cleared his throat, not once but four times. "Hard labor is the general area," he began. "Mining the specific job."

"All three?"

"Yes. It's in their lungs, clear evidence of coal tar, coal dust." He nodded toward "Rankin's" body. "That one even has black lung disease."

"Great! Beautiful!"

"There's more. None of the three died of decapitation."

"We figured they didn't."

"I make it arsenic poisoning."

Doc was thinking aloud. "They were murdered. Of course! They had to be fresh. Corpses to order, tailor-made . . ."

"Well put. You'll no doubt find a tailor involved somewhere along the line."

"I'm not from Texas, Doctor. My partner knows a lot more about this part of the country than I do. Are there many coal mines?"

Fellstone closed his pad and stared past Doc at the wall behind him. "That's what confuses me. I've lived in northwest Texas for nearly thirty years. I've traveled practically the entire state since the war. We've got copper, iron ore, lead, zinc, even tin. But I've never heard of a coal mine in Texas. All the coal's up in Pennsylvania and Illinois, isn't it?"

"This is a big state," said Doc, a hint of desperation creeping into his voice. "There's got to be some coal. Those three couldn't have been brought in from Pennsylvania or Illinois. That's too far away."

"Definitely. If they had been brought in from any appreciable distance they'd have to have been preserved. In dry ice, probably. But the undertakers would have noticed that immediately, the effect on the texture of the skin. They would have suspected something was wrong. And yet all three, three different undertakers in three different towns . . ."

"None of whom knew either of the other two, that's been checked; all accepted total strangers as Grater, Hubbell, and Rankin. Embalmed them and authorized burial."

"You make it sound like you think they're involved."

Doc shook his head, staring out the window at the rain barrel of the building next door, a skin of ice covering its contents. "They couldn't be. The whole scheme begins to get too big, too many people. All the relatives, close friends, employees. Everybody agreed those three were the three managers. Obviously—because who, even a best friend, sees a man stark naked and remembers every detail of his body?"

"But Hubbell was married. . . ."

"Doctor, believe me, those two hadn't slept in the same room probably since their wedding night. Even if Pauline took her look and suspected the body wasn't Wilbur's, she'd keep her mouth shut and go along with the game, considering herself well rid of him. Besides which, she collected five thousand in insurance money.

"That's not important, anyway. What bothers me is this coal thing. You say there isn't one single coal mine in the entire state?"

"I said I've never heard of one."

Doc pressed him further, inquiring if, in view of his sizable collection of books in the office, he might have an atlas, or any book that might possibly show the types and locations of Texas's mines. Fellstone suggested he talk with the Reverend Ernest Dilbock at the Baptist church. In the doctor's opinion, Dilbock was the closest thing to a scholar in the entire town, a man whose head was crammed with information on "everything from the Old Testament to the mating habits of the scissor-tailed fly-catcher."

Doc thanked Fellstone profusely, requested him to prepare his bill, promising to put it through for payment as speedily as possible, folded up the doctor's notes on his findings, and jammed them into his pocket. With a promise of assistance in disposing of the bodies, they left.

29

The Reverend Ernest Dilbock looked like a scholar. His pince-nez glasses were clamped to his bony nose, his sallow skin clearly lacked exposure to wind and weather, his forehead was high and, Doc imagined hopefully, crammed to his thinning gray hair with all the knowledge in academic captivity. In short, a raving bibliomaniac.

The chief shepherd of Amarillo's Baptist flock was standing in his pulpit rehearsing his sermon for the coming Sunday when Doc and Raider walked in, Stetson and derby discreetly removed, introducing themselves as "representatives of the U.S. Bureau of Mines inspecting various installations throughout Oklahoma and Texas."

"Our records indicate that there are no coal mines in Texas," said Doc, his voice echoing over the ranks of empty benches serving as pews.

"That's not entirely true," said the Reverend Dilbock, his position above them increasing the echo's hollowness. "There is one."

"Only one?"

"To my knowledge only one."

Doc and Raider exchanged glances. Launched into explanation, Dilbock was not to be slowed. "Just opened last year, as a matter of fact. Gentlemen, if you'll step this way . . ."

They adjourned to Dilbock's study, a musty, dusty little room walled with books from floor to ceiling. The minister adjusted his glasses and pulled down a map of Texas, its container attached to the top of one of the bookcases, the map drawn concealing all but the two lower shelves. He pointed at a location in the north-central part of the state.

"Wichita Falls!" Raider burst out.

"Just below it," said the Reverend Dilbock. "A little

146 J. D. HARDIN

spot called Pick City. It's not on the map, I'm afraid."
He tapped the map. "But that's the general location."

"Pick *City?*" asked Raider.

"Fewer than a hundred souls, I believe." The Reverend Dilbock sniffed, suggesting disdain. "Not a church in the place, not even a tent chapel."

"You've been there?" asked Doc.

"No, thank you. I rarely leave Amarillo. My duties here at the church are burdensome and endless. I have no time for traveling about. Your coal mine is in Pick City, gentlemen. I know of no other in the entire state."

There followed a lengthy speech on mineralogy in general, recent technological improvements in mining, and hordes of facts and statistics drawn entirely from the minister's head. Doc and Raider listened patiently as reimbursement for Dilbock's welcome good words.

They were rescued by the appearance of a member of the congregation who was requesting assistance of some sort. They started back to the hotel in a jubilant mood, slapping each other on the back, raising their fists victoriously. Suddenly, as they were making their way up the front steps, Raider stopped short, froze, then dodged behind a pillar. He glanced warily up the street. The sun was lowering over the Sacramento Mountains of New Mexico beyond the Staked Plains in the west, flooding the landscape with crimson. But it was another, more ominous red, that had caught Raider's eye and sent him scurrying behind the limited concealment of the slender pillar.

Rouge Floraday, the lady of many reds, of crimson and scarlet, cardinal and ruby and more, was coming down the street. Rouge Floraday, who had wanted very much to become Raider's wife during his previous visit to Amarillo at the beginning of the investigation—and who, when Doc had interrupted their conversation with word that a lady was waiting for "Mr. O'Toole" downstairs in the lobby, had all but clawed Raider's eyes from his head, sending him packing, followed by a string of insults and unladylike phrases that would have burned the ears clean off the head of the Reverend Ernest Dilbock.

"Rouge Whatever-the-hell-her-name-is!" burst Raider. "If she spots me back in town she'll come after me with a

THE SLICK AND THE DEAD   147

shotgun. We got to get us a rooming house, Doc; we can't stay in this hotel. She fucks the whole second floor!"

"Our room's on the third."

"We got to pass the second to get to the third, dammit!"

"Simmer down, we're leaving town anyway. Go down to the stable and get Judith and your horse. I'll pick up the journals at the saloon and our stuff upstairs, check us out, and meet you in back of the hotel in fifteen minutes."

"I just don't want to get married. Not to her. I'd be better off living with a Gila monster. I was lucky to get out of that room alive!"

30

They got out of town as fast as the bay's and Judith's legs could carry them, crossing the Armstrong County line, reaching Goodnight, and taking a room for the night. The plan was to inform the Chicago office of their progress to date the first thing in the morning. Certain minor details would have to be overlooked in the report—failure to inform Pauline Hubbell that the corpse she assumed to be Wilbur Hubbell's had been exhumed without her knowledge, for one. One other oversight had to do with the seventy-five dollars Doc had paid the caretaker. Expenses for Pinkerton operatives in the field were limited to ten dollars a week per man. Doc and Raider agreed to share the expense of the bribe out of pocket. If, as Raider pointed out, they were able to keep their expenses down to eight dollars a week each, they would break even inside of five months.

The oversights in the report troubled Doc, however. But as Raider was quick to point out, if he, Doc, had gone "by the book" in Wichita Falls and requested Pauline Hubbell's permission to exhume "Wilbur,": "The two of us, the whole Agency, and Wells Fargo would see the Gulf of Mexico turn into whiskey before she'd say yes!"

Raider's idea for cutting back on expenses died at birth. As they sat in their hotel room in Goodnight discussing their Pick City strategy, Doc persuaded him that once they got to Wichita Falls, sixteen miles north of Pick City, Judith and the wagon would be stabled and Doc would rent a buggy for the last leg of the journey.

"Why squander money on a buggy?" asked Raider.

"That place down there could turn out to be a hornets' nest. We may have to get out in a hurry. Judith, bless her heart, is just too slow."

"So get a horse."

"And rumpled my coat and trousers? Are you crazy?"

They left Goodnight shortly after sunup, filing their report before departing, adding to it advice to postpone distribution of the photographs of the three suspects obtained by Raider during Doc's sojourn in Wichita Falls and subsequently forwarded to Chicago. Displaying the missing managers on wanted posters would be like waving a red flag. With nearly $300,000 in their pockets they could easily flee the country, and into the unsolved files the case would go.

They ran into a brief snow flurry that turned into freezing rain, three sun-drenched days, and a sleet storm before reaching Wichita Falls.

Even before implementing the initial stage of their strategy, Doc insisted on taking a hotel room so that they might bathe and change their clothes.

One hour later they emerged from the hotel, Raider still attired in the same clothes he'd arrived in—denims, red-plaid wool shirt, fleece-lined jacket, Stetson, and boots.

Doc had changed his entire ensemble. He now wore a nutria fur fedora in place of his derby. He had on his favorite black clay worsted Prince Albert suit lined throughout with the imported black Italian silk. Over it, as protection against the chill, he wore his six-button cassimere overcoat with the black woolen collar.

Visible at the V of the collar was the knot of a paisley print silk four-in-hand. On his hands were silk-lined kid gloves featuring hand-stitched backs, and on his feet were his imported custom Bluchers. Over the Bluchers he wore a pair of buckle snow excluders to keep out the cold.

On their way to the stable, their first stop in town before checking into the hotel long enough to take their baths, Doc tipped his fedora to every woman they passed, forcing Raider to do the same, much to his disgust.

They were greeted at the stable by a flurry of familiar odors. Vehicles stood about outside and inside. The walls were hung with reins and harnesses and water buckets. One corner was piled with sacks of oats, and a stall was filled to overflowing with fresh-smelling hay.

Doc rented his buggy from the stable owner entrusted with Judith's care during the partners' brief absence. The buggy was luxuriously upholstered with a black body, had dark green gears, and was trimmed with an eye-catching gold stripe. It also boasted a fancy canopy top with a full fringe that reminded Raider of tall Winnie's small breasts when it jiggled as Doc climbed up onto the seat to test it for comfort. Out of his apothecary wagon he had gotten his multistripe Princeton wool lap robe, the best of his three robes, placing it over his knees for additional warmth. Between them, Doc and Raider selected a sturdy-looking sorrel to pull the buggy.

Their strategy, discussed and agreed upon on the way over from the hotel, called for Doc to precede Raider to Pick City to permit them to operate independently. They would select a meeting site outside of town and get together and compare notes every night at eleven sharp. In effect Raider would be acting as backup man for his partner.

Doc said his farewells to Judith, a melodramatic exhibition that Raider had witnessed too many times to be amused by. Even the stableman looking on appeared somewhat embarrassed. One would have imagined that Doc was bidding good-bye forever to the woman he loved.

"Good-bye, my little girl. Don't fret and don't be sad, Doc will be back before you know it. I promise, cross my heart." He patted her gently on the head and smoothed her mane, his cheek against hers. "Eat your oats," he rambled on in soothing tones. "Easy on the hay. And don't eat too fast, you know it gives you gas. Don't drink too much water. Be a good girl. Rest up. And promise not to worry about me."

Judith listened, wide-eying him almost fearfully, thought Raider, as if she were debating whether or not he'd had too much to drink for breakfast.

Outside the stable Doc and Raider parted company. But not before Raider got in a parting dig.

"You treat that dumb mule like a damn bride, you silly asshole."

"Judith is not a dumb mule," said Doc coldly, pulling his gloves on a bit more snugly and staring down his nose at his partner. "Had you the benefit of a classical education, I wouldn't have to tell you that Judith of old was a heroine, the slayer of Holofernes."

"Who?"

"Holofernes, King Nebuchadnezzar's general. Judith cut his head off with his own sword."

"That made her a heroine?"

"To the Israelites. Rade, I can see from your face that it's all much too complicated for you. Sometime, when we have two days off back to back, I'll tell you all about it. I can only say that if my little girl, Judith, isn't a true, blue-blooded heroine, with all we put her through, I don't know the meaning of the word."

He climbed onto his seat, removed his right glove, and extending his hand, shook Raider's. "See you in . . . let's make it two days. Sundown Friday."

"Where?"

"Wherever the mine is located, figure one mile directly east of it. Once we get together the first time, we'll know something about the lay of the land and be able to pick a better spot for our eleven o'clock meetings."

"How come you need two whole days?"

"I have to have at least that long to get established, get to know somebody, and be able to get a few answers to questions without arousing people's suspicions."

"I suppose."

"I know."

"Well, good luck."

"Have a good time, rest up while you're waiting. Just be sure you show up sober and with plenty of ammunition."

"Yeah . . ."

Doc waved and away went the buggy, its canopy top fringe jiggling, the little sorrel stepping proudly, head high, the driver tipping his derby to two women heading for the general store.

One of them, noted Raider, a big-bosomed, big-blond, broad-shouldered Amazon in her early sixties, almost seemed to recognize Doc. Hands on hips, she turned and watched the buggy head south out of town.

Raider watched, shrugged, and headed for the nearest bar.

31

Pick City proved to be typical of every mining town Doc had ever passed through. It was alarmingly un-Texaslike in appearance, with its sooty little shacks and a skin of coal dust draped over every foot of the area. The colliery was situated at the far end of the main street, the only street, he decided, reining the sorrel to a halt and looking around.

Close by the shaft cage was the engine house and a larger building, its main floor probably used as an office. The upper floor, considering the building's proximity to the mine shaft, was more than likely in service as a hospital for injured miners.

It was ten o'clock in the morning by Doc's watch. Not a single female was to be seen in the street, and few men. Even as he glanced about a loud whirring and clanking brought the cage to the surface, and off the platform stepped a number of men, all dressed in the same soot-covered overalls and work jackets. All carried lunch boxes. They broke up into small groups as they came up the street toward him.

Again he looked about. It was as if a chunk of western Pennsylvania had been gouged out of the earth, lifted high, and dropped into a hole sixteen miles south of Wichita Falls. In a reflex action, he pulled his lap robe up to within three buttons of his four-in-hand. How any man could keep his clothes halfway clean under such filthy conditions looked to be impossible. But he himself was dressed for a role, and appearances meant everything.

The second largest building in town was the Black Bonanza Saloon. Opposite it stood the Pick City Mining Company store. A group of six men was heading for the store. Doc parked, got down from his seat, and walked up to them. Begging their collective pardons, he introduced himself as "Dr. Stewart W. Harvey of Des Moines, Iowa."

A stumpy man with a game leg and a gold smile eyed him in friendly fashion. "What can we do for you, Doctor?"

"Gentlemen, I'm a friend of the Piggott family of Des Moines. Mrs. Piggott, actually my wife's sister, asked me to come down to Texas to see if I could find Mr. Piggott."

"What did he do, skin out on her?"

Doc nodded sadly. "Harold J. Piggott. He was a coal miner in Pennsylvania at one time, a mine near Hazleton. Mrs. Piggott seems to think he may have gone back to mining. I've been all over western Pennsylvania and southern Illinois. Now here I am. . . ."

"Harry Piggott," mused another man aloud. They all turned the name over in their minds, looking at each other and shaking their heads.

"Never heard o' no Harry Piggott," said the small man. "He could be using a different name, though. What does he look like? Have you got a picture?"

"I only wish I did. That's what's making it so difficult. Harry never had his picture taken."

With visions of a headless corpse in mind, Doc proceeded to create a vague description of Harry Piggott: his height, approximate weight, black hair—the hair on the chest of the corpse being black—muscular build, broad shoulders. His listeners continued to shake their heads.

"That could be anyone of six thousand boys," said one of the group.

"One other thing," continued Doc. "The man I'm looking for was shot in the right buttock." He pointed at his own rear end. "Almost squarely in the center."

"Sounds like Half-ass to me," said the man who had taken the conversation away from his golden-mouthed neighbor. He turned to the man on his other side. "Jace, you remember. Half-ass Munger. He couldn't sit down but on one cheek of his ass on account the other was always sore. He claimed he got shot accidentally and the bullet was still in there."

Jace nodded. "I remember. Sat on half a chair at a time." He looked at Doc. "Tom's right, his name wasn't Piggott, it was Munger or Unger. Something like that."

"Wasn't neither," said the small man. "It was Hungerford."

"It was Munder," said Jace. He was suddenly very certain. Then just as quickly dubious. "Or Unger."

"What was his first name?" asked Doc.

Jace shrugged. "All we ever called him was Half-ass. I don't think he ever did say his first name."

The others nodded.

"I take it he's not around town. . . ." said Doc.

Jace shook his head. "Not no more."

"Would anyone in town know where he headed?"

"That's hard to say," said a fourth man. "Coal fellas come and go. Leastwise 'round here. Come down from Pennsylvania; Rausch Creek, Donaldson, Tremont, Tower City, work a spell, get a little money . . ."

"Damn little," said another man. Everybody laughed. "Twelve hours a day, six days a week, for fifteen bucks."

"Why don't you ask Dink Childs?" suggested Jace. He indicated, his thumb over his shoulder. "He tends bar nights at the Bonanza. Dink knows everybody in town. Everybody coming and going. He's been here since they first opened the shaft. He takes over at ten tonight."

Doc motioned with one hand. "He lives in one of these houses?"

The small smiling man pointed at a two-story house at the end of the street opposite the colliery. "He owns that one. But he ain't to home now. He's been away a couple days. Wichita Falls, they say."

"Who's they?" asked Doc.

"Louie Kimble. He owns the Bonanza. Dink and a couple others tend bar for him," said Jace. "I believe Dink is supposed to be back this evening."

"Do you think Louie would remember Munger, Unger . . . ?"

Jace shook his head. "He only bought in here two or three weeks ago. Took over from the widow Dawkins. Her husband got gunned down by some drunk."

"Gentlemen, I'm most grateful to you. You've given me the best reason for optimism I've had in months. You have no idea how much this means to me. May I show my appreciation by inviting you all to join me in a drink on the house?"

The stampede was small but astonishingly swift. The next thing Doc knew he was standing in the street watching the swinging doors of the Black Bonanza swing.

32

The Black Bonanza was a waterhole like no other Doc had ever seen. The interior resembled a frontier tavern of a century ago. The floor was dirt, the bar a single plank nearly thirty feet long supported by four oil barrels. There was no mirror behind it, no nude lovely framed and fetchingly posed above. Instead a black-and-white print of Adrian "Cap" Anson, stellar first baseman of the Chicagos Professional Baseball Club, gazed down upon the bar patrons. Alongside Anson was a slightly smaller poster displaying muscular Mike McCoole, bare-knuckle claimant to the heavyweight championship title of the U.S. some years earlier.

The walls surrounding also featured well-known bare-knuckle fighters, at least twenty, posed and prepared for combat, including Tom Allen, Sam Hurst (the Stalybridge Infant), and Paddy Ryan, who, Doc recalled, had knocked out Joe Goss in the eighty-seventh round of a battle royal held near Colliers Station, West Virginia, the previous year, thereby becoming undisputed champion.

The one female in attendance was Lily Langtry, whose portrait occupied the bar wall door leading to the side alley. The bar itself was lined with an impressively large supply of whiskey. There were a number of tables and scores of chairs, but no piano, no roulette table, no gaming tables of any type. The lighting was restricted to three feeble kerosene lamps suspended from the ceiling. So dim was it, a man could go blind trying to read a newspaper, mused Doc.

He had been in Pick City since early that morning. It was now five minutes past ten at night. In all that time, strolling about town, caring for his horse and buggy, buying sandwiches at the Mine Store, eating a dinner steak at the Bonanza, he had yet to see a woman.

The bar was half-filled with patrons, mostly miners,

along with two well-dressed middle-aged men whom Doc took to be company officials. Occupying a table alone in the corner in the shadow of the Jersey Lily was an old-timer who, from the sorrowful look on his wizened features as he contemplated his empty glass, turning it futilely, running his finger around the inside and licking it, appeared to be the town drunk.

Doc introduced himself to Dink Childs, a hard-looking man with more than one broken knuckle showing on the backs of his hands. His hair was the color of anthracite and his huge eyebrows lent him a glower that persisted even when he laughed. They talked about the absence of women in the town and Childs explained that none of the miners was married. A number of whores drifted into town from time to time, but they caused more trouble than those running the mine considered they were worth, so now as quickly as they arrived they were sent on their way. The conversation then got around to Harry Piggott.

"Munger, Unger?" Childs thought a moment as he refilled Doc's glass. Then he slowly shook his head from side to side.

"The name's not familiar. . . ."

"Hungerford?"

"Nope."

Doc had repeated the gist of his explanation to the miners.

"They called him Half-ass."

"And somebody in town told you I knew him?"

Doc nodded. "They gave you credit for knowing everybody who's come and gone since the mine opened."

"Who said that?"

"I never did get their names."

Patiently, sensing that he was wearing Childs's own patience thinner by the minute, Doc urged the man to jog his memory. He described the plight of Piggott's deserted wife, adding two children to his morning story, telling Childs how much the man was missed, how marvelous it would be if by some miracle he, Dr. Stewart Harvey of Des Moines, would be able to find Harry and induce him to return to his loved ones.

"I'm sorry," said Childs. "I just don't recall any man called Half-ass anything. Not in Pick City, not anywhere.

I'd like to help you, Doctor, I really would. But I can't remember somebody I never met."

"Of course not." Doc finished his whiskey, paid for it, touched the brim of his fedora in salute, and thanked Childs for his trouble.

"No trouble, Doctor. Come see us again."

Doc thought a moment. "I don't know as I'll be in town long. It's beginning to look like one more dead end."

"Where will you go from here?"

"There's some coal mining in southern Indiana, so I hear. Near Evansville."

"Good luck."

"Thank you."

"Hey, mister . . ."

Doc turned at the voice. A slightly bleary-eyed miner with a well-scrubbed face but both ears filthy where the soaping, rinsing, and toweling had stopped, smirked at him, his two friends behind him looking over his shoulders. As Doc turned toward him, the man looked back at one of the others and winked.

"What are you all gussied up for, you with the circus?"

"Hello, friend," said Doc. "Good-bye, friend."

He started past him toward the doors, but the man caught hold of his sleeve. "Don't go rushin' off. I asked you a question. Are you some kinda preacher?"

"Would you kindly let go of my sleeve?"

The man laughed, but his tone turned surly. "You one o' them big-city pansies come down here lookin' for playmates? Are . . ."

The next question never really got started. Jerking free, Doc drove his right fist into the speaker's stomach, doubling him over so far it appeared his spine was hinged. He sat down hard, his hands clutching his stomach, gasping for breath. Doc walked out without so much as a touch to the brim of his hat to the two men bending to pick up the man with the pain.

Doc had parked his buggy in the side alley. He was on his way down the alley when the side door to the saloon opened, sending out feeble yellow light and revealing the picture of Lily Langtry. The old-timer, who had been sitting in the corner, closed the door behind him.

"You done real good there, son," he said grinning.

"Thank you."

Doc climbed onto his seat. The old man took hold of the horse's breast strap.

"Don't go away. I got somethin' to tell you, somethin' important."

"What?" His disappointment was bringing him close to discouragement, a state of mind he rarely experienced, and never acknowledged to Raider. But dead-end streets invariably precipitated the feeling. He had hit the man, insulting him more out of frustration over Dink Childs's lack of information than anger at the insult.

"You lookin' after Half-ass?" Doc stared. The other nodded. "Like I say, I can tell you somethin'." He paused and licked his lips. "But talkin' gets me mighty thirsty. You buy me a quart o' Rookus Juice, I'll tell you all of it."

Doc fished a dollar from his billfold and handed it to him. "I'm listening."

"Dink lied to you. He knowed Half-ass. They was thick as fleas. Avery Munger was his real name."

"Why would Childs lie about knowing him?"

The old man shrugged. "I only know they was friends. Dink even made him a Sunday suit."

"Dink Childs is a tailor?" Each word came out with exaggerated separation from the one before it. This was the biggest break yet!

"You bet. He musta made suits for thirty fellas or more since he comed here. He's a wizard with a needle and thread. He could make you a suit that'd fit you better than the one you got on."

His billfold still out and open, Doc relieved it of one more dollar. The old man red-eyed him in astonishment as he accepted.

Doc smiled. "Wait here, Mr. . . . ."

"Applegate. Fred C. Applegate."

"Mr. Applegate, allow me to do the honors."

"Huh?"

"I'll go back in and buy you your bottle of Rookus Juice. You can hang on to those two dollars for breakfast and lunch. Just stick here and keep an eye on my horse."

33

The stranger whose spine Doc had collapsed had departed the premises along with his two friends. Customers were coming in in bunches now and Childs was beginning to get very busy. Recognizing Doc, he greeted him.

"Give me a bottle of Rookus to go."

Childs made a face. "You drink that rotgut?"

"They're all the same to my gut," responded Doc, laying a dollar on the plank.

Childs snapped his fingers. "Oh, say, before you go, I've been thinking and thinking on it and, by Jakes, I do believe I remember the fellow you were asking about. . . ."

"Avery Munger."

"Ave. I never called him Avery and I don't recollect his last name. But I remember him sitting down queerly."

"Half-ass."

"Yeah." Two men at the street end of the bar called for refills. "I can't talk now," continued Childs. "Busy."

"How about tomorrow morning?"

"Afternoon. I need some shut-eye. I'll meet you out front here at one o'clock. Okay?"

"Fine."

Childs walked off to serve the two men. Doc walked off in the opposite direction toward Lily Langtry, opening the door, going out, and handing the bottle to the waiting Fred C. Applegate. The old man's hands shook as he all but snatched it from him.

"Thank you kindly, friend."

"Thank *you*."

Mounting the buggy, Doc snapped the reins and backed out of the alley. The last thing he saw as he waved and turned up the street was Fred C. Applegate standing in the shadows under the upended bottle, gulping down the contents as if he were drinking cold water from a canteen.

Doc drove straight to Dink Childs's house, pulled around back, and parked beside a sturdy-looking window-less barn. The house was dark upstairs and down. He stood with his fists on his hips studying the back door and thinking. Childs was involved in the thing all the way up to his overgrown eyebrows. Nail him and the rest would fall into line. Until all the pieces fit.

Feeling the wind against his cheek, Doc considered the job confronting him. He could cover both floors and the cellar in twenty minutes, if he moved fast. Working in the dark wouldn't be easy, but the moon was out and, once he was inside, his eyes would quickly become accustomed to the darkness.

As he expected, the back door was locked, as were the windows at the rear and on both sides. He couldn't chance being seen at the front door, so he concentrated on the back. Getting out a business card for Dr. Stewart W. Harvey, Des Moines, Iowa, he approached the door and inserted the card into the narrow space between the top rail and the frame, drawing it slowly from one side to the other. Then he drew it from the top right corner down between the stile and the jamb, stopping at the lock bolt, reinserting the card below it and continuing down to the sill.

Beautiful! Not a single separate bolt. Bolts posed problems in entering without breaking. Locks no such problems. Restoring the card to his billfold, he removed his gloves, then unfastened his pick ring from his belt. Selecting a pick, he tried it. But the key inserted from the other side blocked his way. He maneuvered the pick, angling it, jiggling it, but was unable to dislodge the key.

Discontinuing his efforts to do so, he removed a slender rod almost three inches long from the pick ring. Then he took from among the picks a shorter rod flattened at one end, and with a hole through it. The other end of the shorter rod resembled a tiny pipe, threaded inside. This he thrust into the keyhole over the pin of the bothersome key. He then slipped the three-inch rod through the hole in the opposite end of the tool at right angles to give him needed leverage.

Next he thrust a pick into the keyhole, wedging it against the bit of the key to keep it from turning in place.

With his right hand, he slowly turned the threader three times around until it gripped the end of the key pin firmly. Removing the pick wedge, he eased up on the pressure and slowly turned the tool, forcing the key to unlock the door.

Doc moved through the kitchen down a narrow hallway past a door that had to lead to the cellar, and reached the front hall. Glancing about the sparsely and cheaply furnished living and dining rooms, he headed upstairs, his weight creaking each step more loudly than the last.

In the first room he entered was a brass bed with an uncovered straw mattress atop it. In one corner stood a small cabinet in use as a washstand, on it a bowl and pitcher. The only thing inside the cabinet itself was a dirty towel.

The second room he went into appeared to be Childs's bedroom, the bed unmade, the top drawer of the lowboy open and filled with socks and handkerchiefs. Doc ran a practiced hand through each of the other drawers in turn, hoping to find letters, a telegram, anything that might tie Childs in with the scheme more securely than accusations in court. He found nothing.

But behind the third door was solid gold. The room was the largest of the three upstairs, occupying the entire rear half of the upper floor. It was Childs's workroom. Two headless tailor's dummies stood against the wall between the rear windows, one with a cloth measureing tape draped around the stump of its neck. At the left, running practically the length of the wall, stood a work table covered with watches and bolts of cloth, scissors, chalk, and a yardstick. Doc counted six bolts in all, two barely started, the others of varying lenghts.

Near one of the windows a hoop-backed chair had been placed in front of an ancient Minnesota Head sewing machine. Neatly lined up along the window sill were spools of thread. An uncompleted man's jacket was laid out on a second table, white basting thread edging the lapels. In one corner stood an armoire, its doors ajar revealing a number of jackets and complete suits.

So Dink Childs was a tailor; so were five thousand other

men. He made suits for the local residents. He'd made a suit for Avery Munger, the man with the bullet in his bottom, the headless substitute for Wilbur Hubbell. But in spite of the obvious, in spite of Childs's first lying about knowing Munger, any case against the man would depend solely upon the testimony of witnesses, or so it was beginning to appear.

What witnesses? A handful of miners? Dr. Fellstone?

It was too shaky, propped up with hope instead of solid evidence. Doc glanced about the room. If only there were some sort of record book with Hubbell's or Grater's or Rankin's names and measurements. But nothing had turned up in any drawer in any room, at least upstairs.

He made a thorough search downstairs, ending up in the kitchen. Nothing he found came close to an incriminating clue. No arsenic, no record book, no correspondence.

Maybe he'd buried the heads in the cellar?

There was no cellar. The door off the hallway leading out of the kitchen opened to a closet, a broom, dustpan, filthy mop, and tin bucket inside.

Sitting down in the living room, he turned the situation over in his mind. Without concrete evidence they would have to get a confession. Dink Childs did not appear the type who would break down easily. Not with a rope swinging in front of his mind's eye.

The moon shining in through the dining room window slanted across a crudely fashioned table in a foot-wide swath that ended at Doc's feet. There was, he mused, one other option. Searching the house in darkness was not the preferred Pinkerton method. Childs had left town before; he could easily be leaving again, maybe soon. Going over every inch of the house in broad daylight, and the shed behind it, certainly ought to turn up something.

Doc rose and made his way back to the kitchen and opened the door. He had one foot outside when what felt like a keg of nails came down on the top of his fedora, sending purple and orange flashes shooting out in every direction, dissolving the bones in his legs and dropping him.

34

Securely tied to Dink Childs's sewing chair, Doc stared upward at his captor. Childs was leaning against his work table, arms folded, a smirk of triumph only slightly softening his grim features.

From the lingering pain actively making its presence felt under his hair, Doc could envision the size of the bump rising.

"Do you mind my asking what you hit me with?" he inquired.

Childs held up both fists clamped together as one weapon. "Don't worry, the soreness'll go away. Life is full of pain; every man has to have his share."

"Who elected you the dispenser?"

"Who asked you to break into my home?"

Doc grinned, more of a wince actually. The pain up top was not lessening in intensity as he had hoped it might seconds after regaining consciousness.

"What are you doing home at this hour?" he asked. "I was sort of figuring you'd work through until closing time. This is a big disappointment."

"It's going to get bigger. I would have worked through till four. But I got suspicious. That's one of my biggest weaknesses. Looking into your eyes when I admitted knowing old Avery, I could see you getting suspicious. I figured you'd leave, come here, and start nosing around. When I spotted your rig out back, I knew I was right. The fringe matches your Prince Albert."

"What's next?"

Childs unfolded his arms, half-laughed, and walked to the nearest window to look out. "It's still a good four hours till sunup. I could kill you and bury you in my barn. . . ."

"I'd guess that's where Munger's and the other fellows' heads are."

163

"Good guess." He picked Doc's billfold up from the table and showed it to him. "You've got cards that say Dr. Stewart W. Harvey, but you're no doctor. You're some kind of detective, aren't you?" He held up his lock pick ring.

"You could say so, yes."

Childs had searched the billfold, but hastily, failing to find the secret pocket concealing Doc's Pinkerton Operative identification card. He hadn't needed it. He could, mused Doc, jump to conclusions as fast as any man.

"Wells Fargo hire you?" Childs asked.

"That's about it. You've been a busy boy, haven't you? Tailoring, tending bar, traveling around, murdering. . . . You killed Munger and the other two."

"By Jakes, you've got me cold."

"Arsenic."

"Very good. How'd you know?"

"All three bodies have been exhumed and autopsies performed on them. It's all over, Dink, you might just as well untie me and . . ."

"What, let you walk away? Mister, if it was all over, what in the world are you doing down here? Not that your showing up is any disappointment. I've got plans for you."

"Before you start something you can't finish, maybe you ought to think about old man Applegate."

"Fred C.?"

"He loves to drink and he loves to talk. Now, if I were to turn up dead . . ."

"Don't rush me. As for Fred C., he won't be doing any talking. He won't be doing anything. He's laid out on two tables over at the Bonanza. There was enough arsenic in that bottle of Rookus Juice I gave you and you passed on to him to kill a steer." Childs nodded. "Now you're catching on. I heard every word between the two of you in the alley. That door with Lily Langtry on it is as thin as paper. When you left the first time and he got up and went out that door instead of the front, I got a funny feeling. You see, I noticed your horse and buggy already parked in the alley when I came on at ten o'clock. When you showed up five minutes later, right away I decided they belonged to you. New buggy in town, stranger dressed to kill . . ."

Satisfied that this closed the subject, Childs volunteered

an explanation of the scheme that had already succeded in bilking Wells Fargo of nearly $300,000. Nothing, Doc decided, short of a bullet, a knife, a heart attack, a pint of laudanum, or a solid brass muzzle could stop the man from telling him precisely how the scheme worked, detail for minute detail. Mr. Dink Childs was much too proud and conceited to conceal his light under any bushel.

Dink's duties were simple and easy to perform, for a professional tailor. The first phase of his involvement had to do with claiming Grater's and the other managers' clothing, shoes, and effects when they arrived by stage. He would then carefully measure the suit and check his figures against those previously sent to him by the individual manager.

Next he would examine his job records and select a previous customer, one whose measurements, including shoe size, most closely approximated those of the manager to be replaced.

Inviting the victim-to-be to his house for a drink, he would poison him, decapitate him, clean up, stop any lingering bleeding with wax, then dress the corpse in the clothing, shoes, and accessories delivered earlier. The body would then be rushed to Amarillo, Wichita Falls, or Clayton, the robbery staged by two co-workers, the wax removed from the corpse's severed neck, chicken blood spattered about the office, and the safe blown.

"The money taken . . ."

"Oh, no, that part of it is handled by the manager himself. He takes it out at the close of business, and that night . . ." Childs winked. "Ingenious, don't you think? Be honest. It was partly my idea."

"Come on, Dink, who do you know has ever had 'part' of an idea? You added window dressing, maybe, and you do your job. But who really thought it up?"

If Childs was insulted, he failed to reveal it. "I'm getting tired talking; it's your turn. How did you get on to us? To me?"

Doc explained, leaving out the details, and neglecting to mention that he had a partner who was following him down—due to arrive tomorrow, a day that he himself would probably never see dawn.

Childs heard him out, his face reflecting admiration. "By Jakes, you're clever. Old Otis told me straight out the plan was foolproof. But anything this involved is bound to split a seam here and there. So you've found me, for all the good it'll do you."

"Otis?"

"Otis E. Wilder. Big business tycoon from New York City. Securities, you know, stocks and bonds. Specializes in gold mining investments. That's where the money's going, into our mine. You're looking at a full partner. In writing."

"Congratulations. Old Otis, as you call him, got the original idea, though, didn't he?"

"He helped."

"Where are they digging?"

Childs was about to tell him when he hesitated, thought it over, and shrugged, as if to say "What difference does it make at this point?"

"A place called Sunstone."

"Never heard of it."

"New Mexico, near Gila, near the Arizona border."

"How does it look?"

"Tremendous. Bigger than any single strike in California. We're all going to be millionaires. All we need is about a hundred thousand more."

Doc shook his head in mock sympathy. "Isn't that always the way with mining, though? You get something good going for you, and you're on the brink of a strike, maybe a bonanza, and you run out of money."

"We're not running out of money. We've got it coming. Ever been to Colorado City, Texas?"

"No. It's down the line from Lubbock, though, isn't it?"

"That's right."

"So you've got a fourth manager in your pocket. One more job."

"The last."

The uneasy feeling that had found occupancy in the pit of Doc's stomach when Childs had earlier announced that he had "plans for you," began to flourish its way through his entire system.

Childs continued. "The new manager's name is Franklin Cole. His clothes and things are due in on the stage tomorrow night. He's young, so they tell me, younger than Grater or Hubbell or Rankin. About your age. Bachelor." He cocked his head to one side and eyed Doc appraisingly. "Just about your size. Let me get my book and check the measurements he sent me."

"I'm curious, how come they send you their measurements before their clothes?"

"It gives me plenty of time to check around and make the best possible selection for . . . you know." Again he tilted his head and studied Doc. "Let me get my book. Be right back. I'll get those ropes off you. You strip down to your long johns. I'll give you a tape and you can measure yourself while I hold a gun on you. If I'm right . . ." He held up his hands measuring the width of Doc's shoulders. "If my eye is as good as I think it is . . ."

Raising a hand in a mute request for Doc's indulgence, he left the room to get his book.

35

Raider rode through Pick City late in the afternoon, pacing the bay with the progress of the lowering sun at his back. Past the colliery he rode, guiding his horse along the side of the rutted road between clumps of mesquite, its shoes clicking against the frozen hardpan.

He estimated one mile distance east of the colliery, swinging about to glance at the structure silhouetted against the circle of sky fire slowly being erased by the upward roll of the earth. The shadows lengthened, blending into twilight. The shade took on a soft rosy hue and an almost reverential silence descended upon the land, as if all the creatures and creations of nature capable of sound were struck mute by the sun's leavetaking.

Then a nighthawk out feeding early, soundlessly beating the air with its dark, rusty-brown spotted wings, flew a zigzag pattern directly overhead. Shrieking once, shattering the stillness, it vanished into a cluster of cottonwoods a quarter of a mile away.

Raider waited. The last few miles had given him a thirst the water in his canteen could never slake. Dismounting, he ambled about stretching his legs. And waited. Then he mounted up and began riding an ever-widening circle search for Doc. Calling. Whistling . . .

"Leave it to that son of a bitch to be late," he said to his horse in a voice suggesting both impatience and anxiety.

Doc was never late. A train conductor could set his watch by his comings and goings. Never late unless delayed.

Raider had not been too impressed with Pick City riding through. But he'd not anticipated anything better. It too closely resembled an eastern milltown impatiently waiting to grow up into another Pittsburgh.

He stared at the tall black man-made mesa, the colliery pushing itself into the darkening sky. He rode in a circle for about an hour before concluding that Doc would not be joining him this night. No word, no message, no hint of the reason for his failure to appear.

It was trouble. It had to be. He wished to hell his partner carried his .38 strapped under his arm, even if he didn't fancy it hanging in a holster from his belt like everybody else. No ready guns for him, though. Whatever fix he got into, his mouth could get him out. So he claimed. Maybe for once in his life, he was dead wrong.

He would ride back into town and look around. Not for Doc, rather for the sorrel and the buggy with the fringe. No need to question anybody, not as long as his eyes and ears were working. If he located the buggy, Doc would have to be close by.

"One step at a time," he said aloud. Spurring his horse, he went galloping away in the direction of the colliery. Riding back through town, he saw no sign of any buggy, let along a black one with a fringed canopy. Nor was he any more successful circling the town. Nothing but a wreck of a market wagon missing both front wheels could be seen.

After tying his horse in front of the saloon, he went in. One man was drinking at the bar, but a dozen others were gathered about a coffin sitting on two tables drawn together at the rear. All had their heads bared, holding their caps and mumbling among themselves.

"Who's the corpse?" asked the patron at the bar as Raider stepped up to it.

The gray-faced older man dispensing the whiskey polished a glass and held it up to examine it. His apron, noted Raider, was as dirty as the curtains in the hotel room in Clayton. Everything appeared dirty in this Pick City, outside and in.

"Valley Tan," Raider said quietly.

The bartender nodded and poured. "That's Fred C. . . ."

"Applegate!" exclaimed the drinker. "Good grief, what happened?"

"Too much Rookus Juice. They found him in the alley practically swimming in it, the empty bottle in his hand."

"Who in red hell would be dumb enough to give Fred

C. Applegate a full bottle of Rookus Juice?" asked the man.

"I'll tell you who," said a voice behind Raider. He turned out of curiosity. The group surrounding the coffin was breaking up, bearing down on the bar. The man who had spoken was a stumpy little miner with a mouth full of gold teeth. "That stranger with the Prince Albert suit, the fancy four-in-hand . . ."

"The one with the buggy with the fringe come to town early yesterday," piped up another man. "Jace Sherman saw him hand old Fred the bottle." He pointed toward Lily Langtry. "Out in the alley. Jace was walking by, glanced in, and saw . . ."

"Where'd that stranger get to?" asked the man beside Raider.

"Nobody seems to know. My guess is he left town in a hurry. Saw what he'd done to Fred C. and ran away fast as his buggy could carry him!"

"He as good as murdered him," said gold mouth. "Jace said it and I agrees. But he could still be in town. We oughta at least look."

They babbled on, everybody sticking his car in it. It had all the earmarks of a lynch mob in the making, thought Raider, accusations against "that Dr. Somebody with the buggy" flying about like gnats in a cantina in July. In the meantime, a newcomer had appeared, pushing through the bat-wing doors and joining the bartender behind the plank.

"You're early, Dink," said the man beside Raider. "It ain't even eight yet."

Raider looked on as the man called Dink poured himself half a shot and sipped it. "I'm not working tonight, Will. Night off. I just came over to kill time till the stage gets in."

The discussion regarding the circumstances surrounding the death of Fred C. Applegate was becoming more heated as it went on. Raider was curious as to how much longer his friends were intending to exhibit the corpse in the saloon before burying it. Another day and another night and it would start becoming less a sympathy and more of an odoriferous annoyance. He finished his whiskey and left. In the street he glanced up and down.

Lights were showing in most of the buildings. Pick City's entire population seemed to be indoors.

So Doc had given some old man a quart of Rookus Juice that had killed him. He'd probably gotten out before the miners discovered the dead man and started after his benefactor with a noose.

Was that the way it had worked? Was that the reason he was unable to find Doc? Maybe, maybe not. If he had skinned out, what was to prevent his showing up for their sundown meeting? Leaving his horse tied in front of the Black Bonanza, Raider walked slowly up the street. Why would Doc give a stranger a full bottle of Rookus Juice? Hardly for the sake of charity. More likely in payment for something.

What? What he'd come to Pick City for. Information. Worthwhile, reliable, at least in his estimation, or he never would have paid for it. He'd learned something and then lit out.

Or had he? One minute he had him leaving, the next not. . . .

Raider's only course seemed to be to search every dwelling in town, every building, everything with four walls. Better yet, first find the buggy.

36

The majority of the outbuildings girdling the town horseshoelike, with the colliery and its building standing at the open end, were unlocked. There were buggies and buckboards and horses in all sizes and breeds. Even sorrels. But none resembled Doc's and nothing with wheels looked like his rented rig with the fringed canopy.

Raider devised a method for inspecting the interiors of sheds and barns that he could not get into. Rather than break their locks or cracks, he found a stick with one end split and put it to work. Locating a knothole in the side of a building, he wedged a match into the split, lit it, shoved the stick through the hole, then ran around to the doors and in the faint glow of the match was able to make out the shapes and sizes of any vehicles parked inside.

The trick was to make his split-second inspection, assure himself that Doc's buggy was not inside, then run back around to the knothole and pull the stick out before the match dropped off into a haypile or onto something equally dry.

It was tedious work and nerve-wracking, saddled as he was with the instinctive suspicion that Doc was in trouble and the longer it took to get to him, the deeper it was becoming. Feeling his way down the shadowed side of a large barn, number eleven on his inspection tour, he found a knothole, fixed his next-to-last match firmly into the split in the end of it, lit the match, and jammed it through the hole, finding and staying on the balance point.

Around to the doors he ran, shading his eyes and peeking through the half-inch gap between them. The light of the match sent enormous shadows climbing to the roof of the barn revealing stalls and hay and tools, a buckboard . . .

And a buggy with a fringed canopy.

He ran back, pulled out the stick, blew out the match, and threw both away, then started for the back door of the house. A faint light, as pale as ale in a glass, colored the two upstairs windows. But he would have had to have been fifteen feet tall to be able to look inside. He tried the back door, found it locked, gave up on it, and decided on a frontal assault. Moving down the side of the house, he was preparing to turn the corner when he spotted a man coming down the street, slowing his pace as he neared the house. Under his arm was a large rectangular-shaped package bound with twine.

It was the man with the bushy eyebrows, the one the drinker alongside Raider had called Dink. Raider pulled back into the shadows, flattening himself against the side of the house. He could hear the man climb the steps, the sound of a key inserted and turning the lock, the door opening, steps going in, the door closing. Coming around front, Raider started up the steps, then hesitated.

Give it a minute or so, he thought, turn over in his mind exactly what he was going to do once, twice. *Make it clean, no holes, no chance for a slip-up.* Moments later he walked up the steps and knocked at the door.

There was no answer. Again he knocked, pounding loudly. Waiting, he heard steps coming down creaking stairs, approaching the door. He eased his .44 out of its holster. Then he turned sideways, leaning against the siding butt of the door facing.

"Who's there?"

"Gene Mason, the shotgun on the stage. Got a package for you."

"I already picked it up."

"I know, I know. But you missed this one. The driver sent me down."

"I'm busy, just leave it against the door."

"I can't do that, mister. If somebody picks it up the company's responsible."

"Okay . . ."

The door opened an inch, one eye and the muzzle of a gun showing. Raider kicked, knocking Childs sprawling, opening the door wide. Childs was sitting on the floor, his palms flat against it, his gun loosed from his hand sliding ten feet away before it came to rest. Stepping inside. Raider leveled his .44 at him.

"On your feet!"

Raider took a step toward him to allow room to close the door behind him. But this simple act, this brief lapse in the full concentration he had focused on the man at his feet was all Childs needed. Bracing himself with his palms as he was, he kicked his heels forward catching Raider full in both insteps.

"Owwwww! Goddammit!"

In an instant they were both down on the floor, Raider having lost his gun, the two of them wrestling, each trying to get a firm grip on the other—any part of the body that would permit the lucky one to get in the first good punch with his free hand. Raider hit, catching his glowering opponent in the shoulder, jerking it back so hard Raider fleetingly wondered why he didn't hear the blade snap.

Childs's right caught him in the side of the head, arousing the dormant pain previously inflicted by Lock Flanagan. By now both men were up on their feet, slamming away at each other with no thought for either gun on the floor, hitting, missing, cursing, moving into the small living room. Raider caught his man full in the heart with a left sending him flying back into a frail-looking wooden chair, splintering it into kindling. Crabbing out of the line of attack, Childs was up on his feet like a shot, brandishing a chair leg, bringing it down upon Raider's head. It glanced off onto his shoulder as he ducked away, all but snapping the trapezius and hurting like red hell. Snatching up another chair, Raider retaliated by slamming Childs over the head, dropping him to his knees. The blow dizzied him; he shook his head, his eyes groggy-looking by the faint light of the moon. But he was only close to out for seconds. When Raider came at him to lift him with a solid left to the jaw, up came Childs's right, catching in the crotch, lifting him off his feet, and sending a broadsword of agonizing pain slicing up through his jewels into his gut, practically up his throat and into his brain.

"You dirty fucking son of a bitch bastard!" roared Raider. "Ill kill you!"

On their feet, they went at each other with a purple vengeance, flailing away, ignoring the exhaustion beginning to set in, slowly draining their power, their quickness, their ability to snap back and retaliate after taking a particularly hard and painful hit They managed to reduce the living room to a total shambles before moving back out into the hall, shattering the bottom half of the stair railing, carrying the action into the dining room and destroying its furnishings just as thoroughly and speedily as they had those in the other room.

This accomplished, they pounded each other down the hallway into the kitchen, beating, belting, slamming, hammering, sustained by neither physical nor nervous energy but the blazing fire of hatred—a hatred so fierce, at least on Raider's part, he felt capable of carrying on for years.

His jewels felt as if somebody had grabbed firm hold of them and twisted them thirty times in the same direction. And was trying for forty. He could almost wish for a straight razor to lop them off his body to relieve him of the agony of ownership.

Each man's face and head were battered and bloodied into masses of red pulp between their necks and their hairlines. Raider tasted blood; blood ran down his forehead collecting in his eyebrows. It dripped into his eyes and partially blinded him, stinging his eyeballs with its salt. The wound inflicted in his cheek by Little Feather's willow switch had been reopened and was spilling its crimson contents down his neck.

Childs spit, relieving his mouth of two teeth. He had broken a knuckle on his left hand and was now working almost exclusively with his right. Raider's own left felt as if at least half of the fourteen knuckles filling his fingers had been shattered. Every time he made contact with any part of Childs, the pain shot up his arm, across his shoulder, practically all the way to his still-sore Adam's apple joining the point of the broadsword driving upward from his crotch.

Never in memory had he fought any man he hated so powerfully as the beetle-browed bastard facing him. Childs was the dirtiest fighter he'd ever seen. Kneeing in close, going for his throat, his eyes, his ears, he obliged Raider to do battle in much the same manner. Closing on Childs in the kitchen, he brought his right leg straight up into the other's crotch, catching his jewels with his shin and precipitating a scream of agony that fairly shook the little house from footings to rafters.

Raider followed up with a right, catching him flush on the nose and flattening it against his face so that twin jets of blood shot from Childs's nostrils, splattering his shirt crimson. Back he fell, his head hitting the front of the stove. Out cold.

His back to the sink pump, Raider dropped slowly to the floor, convinced that every bone in his body was either broken or out of position. And from the sudden wave of weakness sweeping over him like a tent collapsing, the thought arrived that with less than a quart of blood left in his system he would never get up again.

He had, fortunately, more than a quart left, although wiping his face with his hands confirmed that he'd easily lost that much. He caught his breath, resting for a good five minutes leaning against the sink for support. Then he pumped the sink half full and washed his face and head. Childs hadn't stirred. Raider examined the back of the unconscious one's head and ran his fingers over the cast-iron edge of the stove. The man would be out for a week, he decided, but playing safe, he took a towel down from the rack over the sink, ripped it into strips, and tied Childs's hands and feet.

Then he washed his face a second time at the pump, rinsed his mouth out with water, and spit somewhat hesitantly, praying no teeth would emerge. He heaved a sigh of relief when none clicked into the sink and went upstairs.

Sight of Doc in his long johns tied to a chair, a gag over his mouth and trembling like an aspen with the cold caused Raider to burst out laughing. Doc came back at him with a remark muffled and completely indistinguishable. But the look on his face assured Raider that it was anything but a friendly welcome.

"Jesus Christ, look at you. All tied up with no place to go. Look at those long johns, will you. . . ." Exposing the label at the nape of Doc's neck, he read it aloud. "Gentlemen's High Grade English Underwear. Persian wool, silk finish. Size thirty-six. My, my, I am impressed." Doc mumbled angrily, his eyes flashing. "What? I didn't get that." Doc struggled against his ropes. "Oh, you want me to untie you. Why didn't you say so?"

He released him and was about to remove the gag when Doc pushed away his hands and took it off himself.

"You son of a bitch, I've been trussed up like a calf practically twenty-four hours straight freezing my balls off! And you stand there making stupid jokes! Look at you; what happened, a herd of cattle walk over your face? As if you weren't ugly enough. Look at your face, man!"

Doc had gotten up, had finished working the soreness out of his wrists and ankles, and moving Raider to a small unframed wall mirror, showed him his face. Raider took one look and felt sick to his stomach. It appeared he had been fighting against twelve fists instead of two. And had taken every punch in the face. The only unwounded areas appeared to be his eyes and his moustache.

"It'll heal."

"Let's hope you live that long. What did you do with Childs?"

Raider told him, adding a brief description of the brawl. Doc indicated an unopened package on the work table. Raider recognized it as the one Childs had brought home. Doc told him about Colorado City and the proposed fourth and last decapitation. Then he began dressing.

"I was supposed to be it. Lucky me, my sizes practically jibed measurement for measurement with somebody named Franklin Cole, the Wells Fargo manager over there. You got here just in time. The bastard was going to poison me and lop off my head. "Look." Doc pointed to the smaller table. On it was a bottle of white powder, a bottle of whiskey, and a cleaver.

"If I turned down his offer of a drink, he'd just tie me to the table, knock me cold, and zip with the cleaver. He told me exactly what I could expect, step by step. He told me everything."

"So tell me."

Doc did so, answering Raider's questions, asking a few of his own following the big one, how Raider had managed to find him. The air cleared. Doc made a face and shook his head.

"We've got a problem."

"Childs? Don't worry about him. He's out colder than a cave. All tied up in a neat little package."

"It's not him, it's the other two. Two others in the gang, the two who set up the robbery scenes, placing the bodies, blowing the safes and all. They're due to show up here in a couple hours. They're coming up from Colorado City with a fast team and a buckboard to pick up the body."

"That's a hundred-and-eighty miles or more one way."

"They've got it all planned. According to Childs every fifty miles on the way back, they'll switch to a fresh team. When they get here . . ."

"We'll be long gone," interrupted Raider. "With our friend downstairs in custody. He's all we need. At least to start . . ."

"That's no good, Rade. If he's not here prepared to deliver, it'll tip off those two coming."

Raider sat on the sewing chair holding his head between his hands, a headache seemingly capable of bursting his skull into fragments rooting itself in his brain. "What you're saying is we've got to give them a body." Glancing up, he brightened. "What about Childs's?"

Doc shook his head. "It wouldn't work. He's bigger than I am. We'd never get Cole's clothes to fit him. Besides, are you going to be the one to chop off his head for them or do you want me to do it?"

"Okay, so what do we do?"

"Let's talk it out. But first, let's go over to the Black Bonanza and get a bite to eat. I'm starving."

"Like hell. You stay out of that place. Those barfly friends of that old man you gave the Rookus Juice to are aching to get their hands on you and introduce you to the nearest tree."

"Childs poisoned him, I didn't."

"Don't bother trying to explain that to them."

Doc pondered a moment. "I wish we knew the exact procedure—how they pick up the body. Do they come into the house? Does he take it down to the barn? Does he meet them at the back door?"

"That sound most like it," said Raider.

"If we try it and it turns out he doesn't, they'll be suspicious and we'll either be in for gunplay or they'll run for it. If they get away . . ."

"Hold it one second." Raider went downstairs, retrieving both guns and taking a quick look at the unconscious Childs in the kitchen. Then back upstairs he went.

"I think I know how we ought to handle it," said Doc. "You keep an eye out up front. I'll watch the rear. When they show up, if they drive their buckboard down the side of the house, you come back and join me."

"When they come to the door, you open it fast," added Raider. "I'll get the drop on them. No shooting, no noise, no problems."

"Let's hope it turns out that easy."

37

For once in their combined professional lives, a best-laid plan actually came off. Hitchlessly. The two delivery men were captured at the back door at gunpoint, relieved of their weapons, informed of the change in plans, and bound and gagged.

"I'm hungry, I'm thirsty, I could use a good night's sleep," said Raider in a relieved tone. "But most of all I'd like to get out of this town as fast as we can."

"We'll use their buckboard. We can lay them in back. There's got to be canvas or blankets, something in the barn we can cover them with. That reminds me, there's also some very incriminating evidence in the barn. Three human heads."

"Oh, Jesus . . . you don't want to dig 'em up now, do you?"

"Evidence is evidence, Rade. We need all we can get." He hefted Childs's record book. "This helps, but those heads . . ."

"Can't we tell Wagner we're so busy winding this thing up we didn't have time to dig for the heads? We've got to get to the nearest telegraph key so you can alert the home office. They have to get in touch with the law in Colorado City. They've got to grab that manager down there."

"Good point."

They were standing in the dining room surrounded by wrecked furniture. Doc had taken photographs of every inch of the workroom. Stretched out on the kitchen floor were all three prisoners, Childs had not yet come around.

"They were probably planning to pull the Colorado City job tomorrow night," Raider went on. "If we hang around here . . ."

Doc nodded. "Okay. We'll get back up to Wichita Falls."

"You drive the buckboard, I'll follow you. If by this time somebody hasn't walked off with my horse in front of the saloon . . ."

"What about the buggy? It has to be returned."

"Doc, you show that buggy out in the street ten seconds, you're liable to get a bullet in the head. This town is looking for you. Leave the buggy. Thirty-five bucks. . . charge it to expenses."

"By the time we finish this one we're going to have a swindle sheet twice as long as your arm, with half of it unreimbursable. The least we can do is take the horse back."

"I suppose. Let's get moving before sunup."

Doc consulted his watch. "It's not even two-thirty yet. Plenty of time."

They loaded their prisoners, gathered up the package containing Franklin Cole's clothing and effects, the arsenic, the bottle of whiskey, the cleaver, and Childs's book, tied the sorrel to the tailgate of the buckboard, and prepared to depart Pick City. Raider stopped Doc as he was climbing up onto his seat.

"I've got an idea."

"Tell me on the way."

"Shut up and listen. That Prince Albert outfit, that cassimere overcoat and hat . . ."

"Fedora."

"They're a dead giveaway. Even without your buggy. If these boys are out roaming around looking for you, which I wouldn't be surprised at, they'll spot you from half a mile off. Why don't you change into Cole's clothes? They're supposed to fit you."

To Raider's surprise, Doc unhesitatingly concurred. He unwrapped the package in the kitchen and examined the suit.

"Good Lord, will you look at this. A cheap ugly horse-blanket plaid louder than a church bell. Side button shoes that went out of style twenty years ago, baggy trousers . . ."

"Just put everything on and let's get out of here!"

Doc sighed and groaned. "The sacrifices I make for Allan Pinkerton."

38

Raider's own summons to sacrifice was far from ful-
filled as he was to discover when he went to fetch the bay
from in front of the Bonanza. The horse was there and
happy to see him, restlessly pawing the ground as he
approached and whinnying loudly. Mounting was achy,
but no great problem for his mistreated jewels. Sitting his
saddle didn't hurt as much as he expected it would. But
trying to ride, accommodating the jogging motion, returned the broadsword, all but splitting him with pain.
Dismounting, he walked the horse back to Dink Childs's
house, offering the reins to Doc up on the seat of the
buckboard waiting for him.

"You ride," said Raider. "I'll drive. My pride and my
joys just aren't up to a damn saddle. Maybe tomorrow."

"Try sitting a blanket instead," suggested Doc.

"No thanks, for now all I'm sitting are the cheeks of
my butt."

"You ought to stop in and see Dr. Sligh when we get
to Wichita Falls. Let him take a look at you, especially
your face. If it doesn't scare him out of ten years'
growth, maybe he can do a little repair work."

"We can't spare the time. You're forgetting, when those
two in the back don't show up in Colorado City with the
merchandise, the manager down there is going to wonder
what happened. And if he's smart, go right on with business as usual. But when he doesn't show up in Sunstone, Hubbell and the others are going to know
something screwed up."

"This is not proper attire for horseback," said Doc
lamely, running his hands down the lapels of Franklin
Cole's plaid suit jacket.

"What do you care, it's not yours. Let's move on out,
let's find us a wire. . . ."

Doc could be grateful that Dink Childs's house was

182

located at the end of the street, permitting them to get out of Pick City without his having to go anywhere near the Black Bonanza. Astride Raider's bay, leading his partner at the reins of the buckboard, Doc glanced back over his shoulder. The street in front of the saloon was filled with miners, all carrying torches.

"Looks like vigilantes' night," yelled Raider above the rattle of the buckboard's wheels. "Ideal time to leave . . ."

They rode north, following the Arnold City–Wichita Falls spur of the Texas and Pacific Railway, the torches gradually blending into a single soft orange dot of light and vanishing altogether at a curve in the tracks. They pulled up about two miles from town at a pole. With only the moon and stars as witnesses, Doc produced his equipment previously transferred from his apothecary wagon to the buggy and finally to the buckboard, Raider ran up the wire and his key on the seat beside him, Doc began tapping, calling for clearance through Kansas City to the home office in Chicago.

"Cross your fingers the night man's awake," commented Raider.

He was, but it took better than an hour to clear the way and get through to him. Taking advantage of the delay, lighting up a Virginia, Doc encoded a brief analysis of the situation along with suggestions as to how it might best be dealt with at the Sunstone end. Contact established with the Pinkerton night duty man, Doc tapped out his message finishing with a tersely worded command to alert Wagner immediately.

The message was received and acknowledged. Raider reclaimed the wire and they continued on to Wichita Falls. Minutes before the sun introduced the day over the northernmost branch of the Trinity River, they came within sight of the town. It appeared at first glance that the slowly lightening gray sky had met the horizon snugly in a straight line only to have some capricious god snip out a silhouette, squat blocks of black against the gray, with not so much as a single candle in sight to mar the illusion.

Dawn arrived swiftly, the pale sun escaping the Trinity, exchanging it for the dry domain of the heavens. When they reached town, they split up, Doc going at once to the stable to see Judith, Raider pulling the buck-board up front of the Western Union office. It was not yet open. His three passengers, although bound and gagged, were awake and grunting disapproval of being deprived of their freedom.

The marshal's office was also locked. A restaurant was open, and a middle-aged man and his red-haired daughter were serving early breakfast to six tables of customers. Raider killed time over eggs and toast and coffee, five cups of it before he caught sight of Doc at the reins of the apothecary wagon guiding Judith up the street toward the Western Union office. Raider bolted down his remaining coffee, laid a dollar on the table, and ran out into the street.

By this time the marshal had opened his office for busi-ness. Showing him their identification, Doc and Raider introduced themselves to Marshal Whit Burrows, a squat, hog-faced man supporting a belly so ample that his gun-belt had to be slung under it to enable him to buckle on. This placed his .45 out of his sight somewhere close to the inside of his right thigh. But his comical appear-ance notwithstanding, including a half plug of tobacco bulging one cheek, it was clear from the conversation that the man was an experienced and intelligent lawman.

Burrows sat at his desk listening to their explanation, interrupting only to voice some small concern over juris-dictional rights, but upon learning that Wilbur Hubbell, former pillar of Wichita Falls society, was involved, he became eager to cooperate.

"Where do you figger to try this bunch?" he asked in a gravelly drawl, looking from Childs to the two delivery men standing still bound and gagged between Raider and Doc.

"That'll be up to Wells Fargo," said Doc. "But we still have to round up the ringleaders."

"What time does your Western Union office open?" in-quired Raider.

"Eight, generally."

Doc consulted his watch and shook his head. "That's better than an hour." He explained. "We're waiting for orders from the home office as to the next move."

"I can go wake up Clyde Hairston, the operator, and get him to open up early."

"That's okay, you needn't bother. Thanks all the same."

The marshal eyed Childs and the other two. "How long am I supposed to hang on to these boys?"

"Somebody'll be down to pick them up in a day or so," said Raider.

Burrows nodded. "You can take off their gags and bindings if you don't mind." Opening the top drawer of his desk, he brought out a key. Raider untied Childs, last of all removing his gag.

"How're your jewels?" Childs asked him smirking.

"Fine, how's your nose?"

"Couldn't be better. Your face looks great."

"Yours, too."

The three were placed in one of the four cells in the rear. The marshal came back grinning. "They ain't even had breakfast yet and already they're startin' to squabble."

"If you've got nothing better to do, listen," advised Doc. "You may hear something interesting."

Thanking Burrows, they left. At the stable they swapped the buckboard for the buggy left behind, coming out five dollars short on the deal. They also restored Doc's telegraph equipment to its compartment in the floor of the wagon and, tying the bay behind, left town for the nearest pole affording some degree of privacy. As both expected, a message from Wagner was waiting for their call in. Decoded, it proved brief but explicit:

TURN PRISONERS IN W. F.
HEAD FOR S. HELP ON WAY

Doc got out his map, poring over it briefly and announcing that better than six hundred miles separated them from their destination.

"It's us against the clock," said Raider soberly. "Doc, Judith is just too slow."

"I realize that."

"We never should have traded in the buckboard."

"It wouldn't be much faster. We've got mountains, rivers, gypsum flats. Except for the Plains it's hard going all the way. Besides, if we had kept the buckboard we wouldn't have fresh teams waiting for us every fifty miles."

Raider nodded. "I get what you're coming around to."

"You think maybe you can sit a horse now?"

"Oh, hell yes, it's been all of seven hours. . . ." He paused, deliberated, and brightened. "I could ride standing up in my stirrups."

"Six hundred—odd miles?" Doc's tone made it unnecessary for him to shake his head. But Raider clung to the idea.

"We could ride hard for twenty-mile stretches, me on the bay, you on a rented horse. Resting ten minutes every twenty miles. It would work out the same as if we rode at a steady gait."

"Cantering . . ."

"Yeah."

"It might work, if your horse goes along with the idea. You and your pride and joys. Didn't your father ever teach you how to protect yourself?"

"Why don't you shut your mouth? Isn't it bad enough I got to live with pain?"

"Don't mention discomfort to me, friend. You're looking at a starving man. I haven't eaten in two days."

"We'll go back into town," said Raider. "I'll get you a good horse, we'll restable Judith and the wagon, you eat, we'll stock up on some grub. . . ."

"If I'm going to ride a horse, I'm going to have to carry my equipment in a damn paper sack or something."

"We'll work it out, let's go."

39

They followed the Wichita River to Benjamin, riding hard, resting, remounting, resuming the gallop, the bay taking Raider's new technique with visible apprehension at first. By the time they had crossed the Kansas-Missouri and Ohio tracks and had come within sight of the open waters of Duck Creek, it had become accustomed to carrying a man standing in his stirrups. They reined up alongside the creek, Raider dismounting and sitting down on the bank. He pulled off his boots and began massaging first one arch, then the other.

"What's the matter?" asked Doc. He had let his horse loose to graze on the tow-colored grass. There was no snow here, nor any ice; they had ridden out of winter into the southern warmth. Ahead lay the Texas end of the Great Plains and, beyond, the Staked Plains. They would see no more snow until they reached and were forced to ascend the Sacramento Mountains across the border of New Mexico Territory.

The sun was warm, the air comfortably cool descending from the heights of Double Mountain to the south.

Raider sighed and continued his massaging. Doc repeated the question.

"My feet are giving out, my arches."

"Ride standing on your toes."

"I tried. I slip out. My bootsoles are too smooth. . . ."

"How about riding in your socks?"

"With my whole weight on my toes? You crazy? Jesus Christ, I wish we didn't have so far to go! I've been thinking, this could turn out a bigger wild goose chase than running down the pot of gold at the end of the rainbow. What if that manager down in Colorado City contacts Wilbur Hubbell and the rest out in Sunstone and tells them it looks like the roof's fallen in?"

"How would he contact them?"

"Telegraph, how else? To the nearest town and get a message up to them. Doc, we got to figure Cole is no dummy. Not to be manager of a Wells Fargo office."

"Maybe, but what if the corpse failing to show puts the fear of God into him? What if he isn't loyal enough to stick his neck out and warn Sunstone? Right now, with no crime committed, he's clean. Why deliberately incriminate himself?"

"I don't know. What if? What if? Let's cross our fingers he's got more brains than balls. Oooooo . . ."

"What's the matter now?"

"Just saying that word . . ."

Doc sighed. "Goddammit, Rade, I don't like to criticize, but you're getting to be a handful, you really are. Why don't you just climb up on your horse, grit your teeth, make believe you don't have any balls. Pretend you're a female. I'll bet you won't feel a single twinge. It's all in the mind."

"You're an asshole, you know that, Weatherbee? I mean you've got no feelings, no sensitivity; sometimes I think you're not even human."

"Time's wasting. Let's ride."

Recovering his horse, Doc vaulted lightly into the saddle and went splashing through the creek up the other side, galloping toward the Plains.

"Slow down, goddamn you!"

There were more words, but the distance rapidly lengthening between them made it impossible for Doc to hear.

They stayed within a mile of each other until crude signs announcing the impending arrival of the border began showing. They covered upwards of 180 miles by Doc's reckoning the first day into twilight, and stopped for the night in Wary, a few miles beyond Lubbock.

The horses were almost completely blown. Raider felt as if he had been castrated, with the affected area lathered with axle grease and ignited. Doc admitted to being tired.

Raider's chief concern was not the living hell the mad dash to Sunstone was putting his joys through; it was the growing suspicion that they would never again perform for him. Never fill; never again send a load pounding upward to the head of his cock and into a waiting aperture of one sort or another. All Doc's reassurances to the contrary failed to collapse this conviction.

"My sex life is finished!" exclaimed Raider. This announcement was repeated every five minutes.

"I swear to God," he muttered just before lights out in their squalid little rooming house chamber. "If my manhood never recovers, I'll sue the Pinkerton Detective Agency for twenty million dollars!"

"That settles it!" snapped Doc sitting up in bed. "I'm sick and tired of your goddamn endless bellyaching. You can stay here and rest your precious balls. I'll go onto Sunstone alone and finish the job!"

The challenge flung in his face, Raider snapped back with a threat to add to his partner's collection of false teeth. There began a loud argument until a sharp rapping on the other side of the wall and a female voice that sounded like a turkey buzzard in distress ordered them to cease.

40

Three hard-riding days later, shortly before noon, Raider and Doc approached a party of armed men gathered in the shade of a sprawling cottonwood standing forty yards from the girdle of rubble low walling the base of Sunstone Mountain. The mountain rose in challenge to the cloud-cluttered blue sky, a dun pyramid sparsely tufted with scrub oak halfway up its slopes. Above the oak line nothing could be seen growing. Hanging directly overhead, focusing on the summit, the sun flung down its brazen brightness, causing the growth-free smoother planes of the slope to shine like mirrors.

Nearly four hundred feet up, nature had conveniently carved a plateau. Perched upon it was a newly built shack. To the right of the shack a mine entrance beckoned gaping blackly, its perpendicular posts and cross-beam joining them clearly visible from below. From the entrance a set of cart tracks ran down to the base of the mountain. The carts themselves were concealed inside the mine, let down and hauled back up by a windlass.

Joining the others under the tree, Raider and Doc introduced themselves. Four of the men they already knew, Pinkerton operatives whose trails they had crossed. The others included Sheriff Wells Kilgore of nearby Sunstone, a town that looked to Raider from a distance to be only slightly larger than Pick City. With the sheriff were three deputies, two young brothers, Russell and Tom Coombs, and a Mescalero Apache, headband, beads, and all, his skin the color of milk chocolate, and his smile as bright as the sun over Sunstone Mountain. His name was Joseph White Bull. According to Kilgore, who resembled Marshal Burrows in girth and height, but was obviously much older and far more grizzled-looking, White Bull had quit the reservation near Ruidoso in the south-central part of the territory and come west to be with his white mother's people.

For a half-breed, Joseph White Bull spoke wretched English. But the sheriff claimed he could shoot the iris out of a crow's eye at a one hundred yards with anybody's Winchester. Apprised of this, niether Doc nor Raider could bring themselves to fret over Joseph's lack of learning.

Kilgore lit his pipe and, settling his bulk on a rock, his Winchester blanced across his knees, filled the new arrivals in on the situation.

"There's two of 'em up there with the workers. We figure about twenty miners, some locals, some from over the border and up north. They're well armed and well stocked with vittles. To be blunt about it, they could hold off a army division for at least six months. They got like a fort up there."

"Which two?" inquired Doc. "Hubbell? Grater? Rankin?"

"We picked up Rankin in town with some floozie. He's behind bars."

An operative named Leon Haley, ordered down with the three other operatives from Denver, produced copies of the three photographs Raider had sent to Wagner. He held up two of them. "Wilbur Hubbell and Sam Grater, right?"

Doc nodded.

"Accordin' to Rankin, they're up top with the men," interjected Kilgore.

Raider was leaning against the tree trunk looking past the sheriff down the slope in the direction of the little town. A crowd had gathered to watch, at least seventy men, women, and children standing still and staring expectantly.

"We ought to get those people back out of the way," he said.

Kilgore turned and looked. "Curiosity bein' human nature, that ain't gonna be easy, mister. 'sides, some of 'em are part o' this here problem."

"What are you talking about?"

Haley picked up the explanation. "Some of the townspeople have husbands and sons up there working the mine. This is the second day. There's been sporadic shooting. Just before sunup this morning there was a fairly hot exchange. Lasted about two minutes. But nobody's been hit yet. It's a Mexican standoff. . . ."

"Anybody have any warrants for Hubbell and Grater?" inquired Doc.

The sheriff produced two warrants from his back pocket. "All signed and legal-like. We showed 'em, didn't we boys?" Heads nodded. "But o' course they got to be served person to person. We can't get up, they ain't about to come down."

"Have you tried getting up?" asked Raider.

Kilgore sucked on his pipe, spat the fire bite off the tip of his tongue, and angled his face at his questioner. "You see any cover worth writin' home about on that there slope?"

"What about the sides?" asked Doc.

"Same type terrain, same bareness. 'Sides, they got sharpshooters posted ahind good protection." Kilgore jerked a thumb at one of his deputies standing behind him. "Tom here found out, nearly got his ear blowed off."

According to Kilgore the unseen other side of the mountain was little more than a sheer cliff "even a healthy spider'd have a hard time climbin'." The hope was that that night or the one following would be sufficiently cloudy to obscure the moon entering its third quarter.

"If we can get four men started up, two on either side, using the oak for cover. . ." began Haley, running one stubby-fingered hand through his flaming red hair.

"And what do they do if they get up?" asked Doc. "They'll be outnumbered five to one."

Raider had not said a word in five minutes, instead fixing his eyes on the mine entrance and uncovering, examining, and rejecting ideas on how to take it. He concluded that nothing or nobody could. The only feasible solution to the problem was to persuade Hubbell and Grater to give themselves up.

"I think we should send up a man with a white flag," he said finally. "Parlay and talk them into surrendering."

"We tried that," said Kilgore.

Haley nodded. "I went up. Somebody put a shot squarely over my head, so close I could almost feel it parting my hair." He pointed to a scrub oak clinging to life directly below the shack. "See that white spot? That was my flag of truce."

"As far as I can see, we can either sit here til doomsday or blow up the whole goddamn mountain," said the sheriff morosely. "And me an' my boys can't sit here forever. We got the peace to keep in town."

Doc had been sitting on the ground aimlessly picking at dead buffalo grass and listening. He got to his feet.

"You did say blow up the mountain. . . ."

"Mister . . ." began Kilgore.

"Listen, please. We can't get up there day or night. They come down. So why don't we get ourselves something bigger than six guns and Winchesters and blow them out? Where's the nearest fort?"

"Bayard, over by Silver City," said Kilgore.

"Cavalry, it must be . . ."

"Would they have any cannon, I wonder?" asked Haley.

"They got one," piped Tom Coombs, grinning self-consciously. "An old six-pounder from the war. It sits out by the flagpole between two piles o' shells."

"Do they ever fire it?" asked Doc. "Is it on a cradle? It must be."

"I think they used to fire it," Tom continued, "for dress parades and things. But it's old as the hills. They painted it black 'cause it was starting to rust away."

"How far is Fort Bayard?"

"A little over twenty mile," said the sheriff. "We can sure enough ride over and ask the lend o' it."

"With plenty of ammunition," said Raider.

Kilgore scratched his chin and tapped the orange ashes out of his pipe against the side of his boot. "I hope this ain't gonna turn into no slaughter."

"Nothing of the kind," said Doc. "We want Hubbell and Grater just as alive as you want the Sunstone men who are up there. All the cannon's for is to put the fear of God into them. Hopefully scare them down."

Kilgore got up, pocketed his pipe, and addressed Tom Coombs. "You and Russell borrow a buckboard and go over and get that thing. On second thought, make it something heavier, like a four-spring wagon. Tell Colonel Rossbeck what we need it for. Here . . ." He handed both warrants to Tom. "Show him these and the pictures the fellas here give us. Explain the whole shebang and get back quick as you can."

The two deputies were up on their horses and off, heading southwest in a dust cloud that quickly cut off sight of their departure.

"Figure two hours," said Kilgore. "And since this is getting to be idea time, I got one o' my own. I say we blow up the shack. There won't be nobody in there or anythin'. We long ago figgered they's got to be a back entrance which opens directly into an offshoot o' the adit. So's they was able to clean the place out seconds after we started shoutin' and shootin'."

"How can you be absolutely sure Hubbell and Grater are up there?" asked Doc.

"I can't. It's Rankin claims they be."

"Did Rankin mention any other names? Wilder . . . Otis Wilder?"

Kilgore shook his head. "Don't sound familiar. Joseph?" He turned to White Bull. The Indian also shook his head.

"He's the ringleader," said Doc to Haley. "According to the information we got, he's pulling all the strings. Sitting snugly and comfortably in New York City doing it."

"Does Wagner know?" asked Haley.

"Yes, hopefully they've got Wilder under lock and key by now."

Again Raider glanced up at the shack. "I sure would like to get this buttoned up today," he said wistfully. "I'm so tired I could sleep for six weeks."

The cannon arrived in the middle of the afternoon, a cast-iron breech-loading monobloc gun with the date 1855 stamped on each trunnion. Tom Coombs had returned with detailed instructions on how to fire it. It was aimed at the shack, loaded and fired. The shell hit short, scarring the face of the slope thirty feet below the shack, gouging out the perfect representation of a bursting star.

The muzzle was raised. The second shell was fired, but never left the cannon. It blew it apart, killing Tom and seriously injuring two of the Pinkerton operatives standing behind him.

41

Kilgore was livid, close to frothing at the mouth. For the better part of the first hour following the tragedy, he paced up and down under the tree smashing his fist to his palm and muttering, repeating the dead boy's name over and over. Doc tried to reason with him, but it was almost sundown before the sheriff was able to get his emotions under control and talk to him without shouting. Still he made no attempt to conceal the raw edge of anger to his voice and the fury in his eyes. He wanted out of the situation, claiming he had no more stomach for it.

"This is your goddamn nest o' fuckin' eggs, not Sunstone's, not this sheriff, not my deputies, what's left of 'em."

"It was an accident," said Doc for the dozenth time, aware of the undisguisable lameness of his tone.

"Tell that to his folks. To his brother!"

Tom Coombs's body and the two injured Pinkertons had been driven back to town by Joseph White Bull in the wagon borrowed to bring the cannon from the fort— leaving Kilgore the only local man at the scene along with the four remaining operatives.

"Sheriff," said Leon Haley, "these men have got to be captured and taken in. It's our job. We're asking your cooperation, not demanding it. If you feel——"

Doc cut in. "Kilgore . . ." The sheriff jerked about and stared at him, ostensibly unaccustomed to being addressed by his last name. He then turned away. "We didn't kill the boy," Doc went on. "If they weren't up there doing what they're doing, we wouldn't be down here trying to think up a way to take them out of circulation. They've already murdered three innocent men."

"Four!" snapped Kilgore.

Raider placed a hand on Doc's shoulder. "Nearly five, counting this one."

"All we ask," continued Doc, "is that you not let this unfortunate incident sour you on helping us. We really need you. You, your deputies, anyone in town who's willing to pitch in."

Kilgore waved a hand in front of Doc's face. "It ain't Sunstone's problem, can't you get that through your head? I couldn't get three men together in a posse if I paid 'em!"

They talked further. Doc was at his persuasive best, mused Raider, listening and looking on. He could be a real charmer when circumstances forced the role upon him. Kilgore cooled down to the extent of apologizing for his behavior. He and the four operatives ate cold dinner under the tree, beans, biscuits, and hot coffee brought up from town in two Mason jars.

Raider came up with a strategy for taking the mine, explaining it enthusiastically to everyone. "If I can talk to Joseph What's-his-name . . ."

"White Bull," said Kilgore. "Go ahead. But don't ask me to talk him into doin' what he don't want to."

"I won't. I promise."

Twenty minutes later, Raider sat at a corner table across from Joseph White Bull in the Silver Spur Saloon explaining his idea. Joseph was still shaken by the death of Tom Coombs and seemed leery about listening to the stranger with the beat-up face. The music pounded out of the piano by a frail, middle-aged man wearing a patch over one eye sounded as solemn as church to Raider. An air of restraint seemed to have captured the men and women in the saloon; there was little laughter and no singing. The people of Sunstone were obviously shocked and saddened by the tragedy. Raider had bought a bottle of bar whiskey, pouring Joseph White Bull's for him, then his own and setting the bottle down closer to his quest in a hospitable gesture.

"We need a man with an eagle's eye who can shoot an arrow as high as the shack ten times out of ten."

"Not me," said Joseph shaking his head. "I ain't even pick up a bow in that high." He held his arm straight out, palm downward.

"You're a Mescalero. Mescalero braves are supposed

to be very good with a bow, good as the Comanches and the Cheyenne. You came from the reservation. . . ."

"Long time back."

"Don't you know one or two braves back there who can get real distance with accuracy?"

Joseph nodded. "More. Six or seven men can take eye out of buffalo far." He swept his arm in a wide semicircle. "But no good, no good."

"What do you mean?"

"They come off reservation for Joseph White Bull. Joseph White Bull no go to reservation to talk." In his halting English he clarified his point. He had left his people at fifteen. He was now twenty-six; he had never been back. Upon leaving he had headed for Three Rivers. In time he had drifted to Garfield, Hurley, and other towns. But the reception accorded him was always the same, ranging from subtle prejudice to outright hostility. Whatever job he was able to get he would invariably lose to the first white man who came along looking for work—until he had wandered into Sunstone and Wells Kilgore had deputized him, despite the blatant resentment of half the townspeople. Now, after four years, Joseph White Bull had become a fixture. And for the most part, people looking at him had become color blind. To Raider, Joseph almost made himself sound like the local freak. difficult to accept at first. grown used to, tolerated, but generally ignored.

"I am breed who look like full-blooded Indian," he said in a self-conscious tone. "Most breeds look . . ."

"Half and half. Are you satisfied to stay in Sunstone? I mean after four years of people looking through you."

"I stay for Wells Kilgore, for nobody else. Wells man with big heart." He tapped his own. "I be best deputy in Territory for Wells. I do what Wells tell me. If he say 'Joseph, go back to Reservation and find best bow, sharpest eye, greatest far,' I go."

"But you'd hate going back, wouldn't you? Even for fifteen minutes."

"Mescalero treat all breeds like dogs." He spat, then drank. "My own people, white man same; Joseph in between. Half-half, nothing-nothing."

"Never call yourself nothing, Joseph. You're something; you're a man. Brave, loyal. Kilgore calls you his

friend; you call him yours. Any man in this world who
can boast of having one true friend is ahead of the
game."

From the look in his listener's brown eyes, Raider
guessed that his compliment, though well intentioned, was
not wholly understood. Joseph was thick, and very slow;
no education, probably not even basic guidance from his
elders. But along with being loyal to Kilgore, he was
trustworthy, reliable, and no doubt capable of showing
more courage under fire than the average man, red or
white, thought Raider. An asset to the town, even if the
town was too stupid to recognize it as such.

"I can't ask you to go back there. But is it possible
there's somebody from some tribe around here who can
really handle a bow?"

Joseph thought a long time, his chin wrinkling ab-
surdly, pushing up against his lower lip, the corners of his
homely mouth drooping. He stared into his glass, pushing his mind against the problem and holding it there
with an effort that showed in his chin, in the hunch of his
shoulders, in the blanket of silence in which he had
wrapped himself.

"He'd be well paid," said Raider hopefully.

"No Indian want white man's dollars."

"Then we'll buy him something he can use."

"Crooked Arm."

"Huh?"

"Crooked Arm. Old warrior." He touched his left arm.
"Arm broken, crooked. Crooked Arm. Gila." His index
finger went to his jugular vein. "Neck shot antelope. Ten
times no miss. Far, far . . ."

"How far, four hundred feet?"

"Six hundred."

Raider stood up, handing the bottle to Joseph. "We'll
go outside and you show me five hundred."

Outside the swinging doors, Joseph raised his hand in
the direction of the mine. "Up over shack, over mine
from ground . . ." After swigging from the bottle, he
wiped the top with his palm and pushed it at Raider.

"Keep it, just don't get loud drunk. Kilgore wouldn't
like that. This Crooked Arm, where do we find him?"

"Up near Buckhorn."

"What do you think he'd want for the job?"

"Lightning."

"Lightning?"

"In bottle."

"Taos Lightning?" Joseph nodded. "Good, you get him. He does the job, we'll give him big box full of Taos Lightning. Twenty bottles, more. Now tell me all you know about him."

Joseph could add very little apart from praising Crooked Arm's prowess with the bow. Then he proceeded to pull the wooden sidewalk out from under Raider's feet, admitting offhandedly that the last time he had seen Crooked Arm pull a bowstring was eleven years earlier.

"How old is he?"

"Old . . ."

"Jesus Christ, how do you know he can still lift a fucking bow, let alone get an arrow off with any accuracy!"

"Gila warrior like Mescalero. Born with eye of eagle, strength of bear, never lose. . . ."

"Is he as old as Kilgore?" asked Raider clenching his teeth and preparing to wince at the answer.

"He less old than Wells."

Raider weighed the situation. "Don't you know anybody younger? Think."

"Mescaleros. They old like Crooked Arm. Younger braves all shoot guns. No more bow and arrow."

"Okay, you know the terms. One case of Taos Lightning. Get your horse, ride up, and tell the sheriff what you're up to and go get Crooked Arm."

42

Kilgore graciously donated his office for the dangerous preparations Raider's inspiration required. It was as typical a lawman's office as the Silver Slipper was a saloon: gun rack, desk, a Globe Lightning stove, wanteds weighing down a bulletin board, and two cells in the rear, one occupied · by Peter Rankin. Rankin demanded to be moved to a safer building as his legal right while Raider and Doc worked. Kilgore locked him in a hotel room with Russell Coombs standing guard at the door. The sheriff himself left his office to the two operatives, Doc insisting that Leon Haley and the other Pinkerton likewise stay away.

Securing a quantity of dynamite, they planned to, as Raider phrased it: "whip up a batch of nitro."

"I've seen it made," he said reassuringly. "It's easy as pie."

"It's also dangerous as hell," said Doc, casting a worried glance at the half-filled box of dynamite sitting on Kilgore's desk.

"Let's see, have we got everything? Pots, gallon can, cheesecloth, dynamite, wooden spoon, small funnel, six two-ounce bottles with corks. We'll only need four, if we're lucky two. But a couple of spares can't hurt."

The pot of water atop the stove began simmering. "I believe the water's hot enough. Set it on the floor, then help me crumble these sticks into the other pot. We'll need at least thirty-five or forty. . . ."

The process Raider had witnessed in the Selkirk brothers' hideout was duplicated step by step. Doc was sweating like a blown stallion, droplets the size of pearls excaping his brow and running down, soaking his face. His cheeks became whiter and whiter while his face took on the aspect of a man doomed to the firing squad at the critical juncture—between the last puff of his smoke and the blindfold.

"Look at your hands shake," Raider admonished him. "Hold 'em steady."

"Shut up! You've already been through this once, I haven't. Don't tell me you weren't nervous your first time."

"I was cool as ice. You look like you're going to have a heart attack."

"Shut up or I swear to God I'll walk out the door and you can finish the job yourself!"

Raider shut up. After what seemed like eons to Doc, they reached the final stage. Raider poured the liquid carefully extracted from the lethal mush into the four small bottles.

"Fill them to the top," cautioned Doc. "Don't leave any room for sloshing."

"Just quiet down and keep your eye on the expert."

Raider finished with a loud sigh. The bottles were gingerly corked and set well back on the desk. Both men sat down to catch their breaths. Doc got his silk handkerchief out and was wiping his face and neck.

"What's on the other side of that wall behind the desk?" asked Raider.

"An alley. No boulders, no snow."

Raider thought a moment, then got up and removed the bottles one by one, cupping one hand underneath each for safety's sake, setting them on the floor. He pulled the desk six inches away from the wall, then returned the bottles to it.

"No sense taking unnecessary chances."

He was talking to himself. The moment he began removing the first bottle from the desk, Doc got up from his chair and without a word walked out.

43

Wells Kilgore had seen sixty and waved it by, in Raider's estimation. Crooked Arm may not have been as old by the calendar, but he looked as if he had ten years on the sheriff. The skin of his face and neck resembled a dried prune, lighter in color perhaps, but as plentifully furrowed. When he opened his mouth to laugh, Raider counted one tooth. The muscles of his left arm were withered and he was unable to straighten it. With a fair-sized stone balanced on each puny shoulder he would have cleared 10 pounds on the nearest platform farm scale. But old as he looked, toothless and puny, wrinkled and ready for the grave, the impression conveyed was that of barbed wire tightly bound and squeezed into the shape of a man.

He had arrived in Sunstone with Joseph White Bull some three hours past midnight. He smelled like he'd been drinking for three straight days, but he walked without weaving, talked without slurring. Joseph had explained his mission to him, and although he spoke no English, he appeared to be enthusiastic and prepared to go to work.

The group had assembled under their favorite tree, Kilgore, two of his three deputies, Raider, Doc, Leon Haley, his companion, and six additional Pinkertons who had arrived from Denver 15 minutes before Joseph's return with Crooked Arm.

The moon was out, but the sky was crowded with fleecy blue clouds and one after another slid across the face of the moon blackening the landscape and the mountain towering above it. By the light of the visible moon, the shack, the entrance to the mine, and the cart tracks could be clearly seen. There were no lights, no sign of life in the area; there had been none since Raider and Doc had gotten there. But the sheriff and Russell

Coombs had seen faces peering out of the darkened entrance, and when Leon Haley had started up with his flag of truce, both sharpshooters positioned left and right above had opened fire, one briefly revealing the top of his hat.

Whoever had designed the site had obviously done so with an eye to holding off any possible attackers from below. Each of the sharpshooter installations, although only large enough for one man, appeared to be accessible from the mine proper so that the men could be replaced every fifteen minutes without the slightest danger of exposure to anyone below.

"He'd get a better shot if he shoots by moonlight," commented Kilgore.

"So would the sharpshooters," said Doc. He turned to Raider. "I wish we could see him try a couple of shots off in the other direction, though. We could see his distance, we could see how accurate he is. . . ."

Raider shook his head. "He's already said he can do it. We've got to take his word for it. You've seen him talking to Joseph. He thinks he's pretty big shakes. If we ask him to prove how good he is, he'd be insulted. He'd likely back out. You know Indians. . . ."

"He's not about to back out of twenty bottles of Taos Lightning," said Haley. "Did you see his eyes light up when the deputy reminded him?"

Doc moved to the tree trunk, leaned against it, and glanced up at the mine. A gentle breeze was coming from the summit, a wayward remnant of the heavy winds propelling the clouds high overhead. "Thank God for the clouds," he murmured. "I only wish there were more. Who's got the arrows?"

Russell Coombs stepped forward holding four of Crooked Arm's Osage orangewood arrows, each with a bottle securely tied to the top of its shaft under the head. Raider took them from the deputy.

"The additional weight is going to affect his accuracy," said Doc. "He's going to have to compensate. Joseph better tell him . . ."

"He knows, for chrissakes!" snapped Raider.

"Make sure. . . . Joseph." Doc beckoned to the deputy and explained to him. Joseph assured him that Crooked

Arm was aware of the problem. The Gila came up behind him, his longbow in hand, checking the upper nock of it.

Raider was staring at the sky. A cloud was approaching the moon. It eased over it. "Let's go. Cover us, everybody. The best you can!"

He and Crooked Arm moved swiftly to the largest boulder at the base, Raider holding the arrows directly in front of him, loping smoothly, biting his lower lip, praying he wouldn't trip. They reached the boulder, crouching. He handed an arrow to Crooked Arm.

"Now, before we lose the cloud. The shack . . ." He pointed upward at it, vaguely discernible in the darkness, and pantomimed shooting. Crooked Arm nodded, grinned, aimed, and let fly. The moon reappeared just as the arrow struck. It was the destruction of the Selkirks' shack duplicated. The explosion lifted it straight upward, roof and four sides separating, the mountain and the ground trembling. Even as the first arrow hit, Crooked Arm was fitting the second to his string, pulling back, bringing the bow ends to within a foot of each other . . . and releasing. The arrow threaded the needle's eye, striking the target dead center, a foot above the crossbeam crowning the mine entrance. The explosion snapped the beam and brought a small avalanche of stone crashing down, all but plugging the entrance completely. Crooked Arm shouted triumphantly and Raider was forced to pull him down behind the boulder out of sight of the sharpshooters.

He needn't have bothered. Within seconds, first one rifle, then the other came clattering down the slope, the men rising from their hiding places, hands high. A white flag appeared at the hole in the pile of rubble at the entrance waving pathetically. A voice called: "We give up . . ."

44

Success is one of nature's unaccredited healers. It speeds recovery from illness or injury with the unique medicine of personal satisfaction; it swells the pride; it strokes the ego inspiring it to enlarge considerably; it rosies the present and the future; it eradicates the tribulations of the past. Basking in the warmth of its direct rays, Raider and Doc had been back in Wichita Falls for three days, Doc to be reunited with Judith, Raider to rest and fully recover from his unfriendly introduction to Dink Childs.

No successful person goes unaware of his success, but the sensation, the warmth of the direct rays become stronger when authority acknowledges and applauds the success.

A congratulatory letter from Allan Pinkerton himself arrived. With it came a wire from Wagner tying up the loose ends. Following the appearance of the white flag, the rubble was cleared by those inside, everyone in the mine was ordered to follow the example of the sharp-shooters and throw down their arms, and clattering down came the arsenal. Hands raised, Wilbur Hubbell and Sam Grater had led their men down to surrender.

According to Wagner, Otis Wilder had been taken into custody by operatives attached to the New York office. Among other crimes, he was charged with complicity in triple murder. The two buckboard drivers engaged to whisk Dink Childs's corpses about Texas and New Mexico could look forward to five to ten years. Childs would undoubtedly hang. Grater, Hubbell, and Rankin, along with Kingpin Wilder, would receive twenty years to life. Franklin Cole, although technically innocent of any actual wrongdoing, would nevertheless be tried and probably given two years' probation for his "intent" to commit a crime. The evidence against him was his suit, which Doc had sent on to the Chicago office.

He and Raider stood in the Western Union office reading, exchanging, and rereading Allan Pinkerton's letter. It
was midafternoon of the mildest winter day of the new
year, the sun pathing the floor with its golden warmth, the
chill absent from the air, the hickory standing outside the
window threatening to bud. The two had just gotten off an
answering wire to Wagner.

"I've never been so glad to see a case wind up in all my
life," announced Raider solemly. "I feel like a new man."

"You look like one. Your face is healing."

"My downstairs is, too—one hundred percent. Doc, do
you realize we can take a couple weeks off and loaf?
Drink . . ."

"Says who?"

"Nobody has to say. It stands to reason. We cleaned up
the biggest case the Agency's had in years. Wells Fargo
lost close to three hundred thousand. And winds up with
legal rights to a damn gold mine that's got to bring in ten
times that. They're happy, the Agency's happy. Hell,
we'll probably get bonuses!"

"Mr. Weatherbee?"

The clerk behind the counter looking out from under a
mass of corn-yellow hair stared at Raider. Raider nodded
at Doc.

"Another telegram for you, sir."

Doc read aloud:

AGAIN CONGRATULATIONS STOP AP QUESTIONING
EXPENSE ACCOUNTS SUBMITTED BY YOU STOP
REIMBURSEMENT DELAYED PENDING CLARIFICATION
STOP

"Jesus Christ!" snapped Raider.

"Wait, there's more."

PROCEED AT ONCE TO GLASGOW MONTANA STOP UPON
ARRIVAL CONTACT OVERTON GREAT NORTHERN
RAILWAY STOP FIF*

"Glasgow, Montana!" exclaimed Raider. *"Glasgow,
Montana!"*

* further information forthcoming

"Sssssh, keep it down."

"Count me out!"

"Rade . . ."

"Glasgow, Montana's about four feet from the Canadian Border. Do you know that? You know how cold it gets up there? Do you know it's February. . . ."

"Rade . . ."

"Gentlemen," began the clerk, gesturing in favor of a more restrained exchange. Raider whirled on him glaring.

"Do *you* know how cold it gets up there!"

Two women standing at the opposite end of the counter gaped at them. Doc grabbed Raider by the arm and pushed him through the open door onto the sidewalk.

"Will you for chrissakes lower your voice?" he rasped.

"I'm not going!"

"It's an assignment. Wagner . . ."

"Screw him!"

Doc walked him off, trying unsuccessfully to placate him. But Raider was getting angrier by the second, swinging his arms, his face reddening, his legs taking on a bowed look, as if he were subconsciously favoring his pride and joys.